RIDING AFTER RUSTLERS

Kate set the alarm clock. "We'll leave before dawn," she said, pulling on a jacket and boots. "I'm going to go call Dad."

"We shouldn't ride bareback," Carole suggested after Kate left.

That made sense. This wasn't a pleasure ride. This was serious business. The lives of many horses could be on the line.

A minute later Kate reappeared. Her face looked grim.

"What's the matter?" asked Stevie.

"The phone's dead. The storm must have knocked it out," Kate answered. "It looks like we're on our own."

THE SADDLE CLUB
SUPER #3

WESTERN STAR

BONNIE BRYANT

A SKYLARK BOOK
NEW YORK · TORONTO · LONDON · SYDNEY · AUCKLAND

RL 5, 009–012

WESTERN STAR
A Skylark Book / November 1995

ISBN 0-553-48270-X

Published simultaneously in the United States and Canada

Bantam Books are published by Bantam Books, a division of Bantam Dou-
bleday Dell Publishing Group, Inc. Its trademark, consisting of the words
"Bantam Books" and the portrayal of a rooster, is Registered in U.S.
Patent and Trademark Office and in other countries. Marca Registrada.
Bantam Books, 1540 Broadway, New York, New York 10036.

PRINTED IN THE UNITED STATES OF AMERICA
OPM   0 9

For Amy La Roche

"THERE!" LISA ATWOOD declared as she folded a dishtowel. "I've dried the very last pot. And put it away. *Now* can I go call Stevie and Carole?" she asked her mother.

"Of course," her mother said. "Just as soon as you—"

"See you later, Mom!" Lisa said, running up the stairs. She suspected her mother was teasing anyway. Mrs. Atwood knew Lisa was dying to talk with her best friends, Stevie Lake and Carole Hanson. There was exciting news to discuss—Christmas was less than a week away and she'd just learned that she and her friends were getting a *wonderful* present!

Lisa blessed the miracle of three-way calling as she dialed her friends' numbers. It saved so much time

1

when she wanted to talk with Stevie and Carole at once.

The three girls had been best friends from the moment they discovered what they had in common. They were all horse-crazy. They were so horse-crazy that they'd invented The Saddle Club for themselves. It had only two rules: Members had to be horse-crazy and they had to be willing to help one another out. The first part was easy. The second part had sometimes been hard, but it was almost always fun.

Lisa thought it was a good thing that the three of them had a strong common bond in their love of horses, because in almost every other way, the girls could not have been more different.

Lisa was studious and methodical. Stevie claimed that Lisa's report cards were dull because the only letter on them was A. Stevie's report cards were much more interesting than that! It wasn't because Stevie wasn't smart. She was very smart; but even she admitted that she could be lazy. Most of the "interesting" parts of Stevie's report cards were penciled notes in the "conduct" section. She had a nose for trouble—and was always getting into it. Fortunately, she was almost as good at getting out of it.

Carole Hanson was the best rider of the three. She'd taken up riding as a very young girl, when she and her family had lived on various Marine Corps bases. When she was ten, they'd moved to the town of Willow Creek,

Virginia, not far from Quantico, where her father worked. She had lived alone with her father since her mother's death from cancer a few years earlier. Carole had decided long ago that she would work with horses when she grew up. The only problem was that she kept changing her mind. One day she was going to be a horse trainer; another day it was a breeder, an instructor, a grand prix rider, or a vet. Some days it was all of them. Horses were her life.

The three girls rode at Pine Hollow Stables in Willow Creek. Pine Hollow's owner, Max Regnery, was their instructor and Pony Club director. Stevie and Carole owned horses and boarded them at Pine Hollow. Stevie's was a big, frisky mare named Belle. Carole rode a talented bay half-thoroughbred gelding named Starlight. Lisa rode Pine Hollow's horses. At the moment she was working with an ex-racehorse named Prancer. Lisa was the newest rider of the three, and she found that learning to ride on a variety of horses was helping her improve fast. Prancer still had a lot to teach her.

The three girls had started The Saddle Club, but they weren't the only members. They were just the only members in Willow Creek. They thought of their other horse-crazy friends as out-of-town members. The out-of-town members included Stevie's boyfriend. His name was Phil Marsten. He lived a few towns away and belonged to the Cross County Pony Club. Two other out-of-town members lived almost all the way across the country. They were Kate Devine and Christine Lonetree. The Saddle Club didn't think they got to see anywhere near enough of them, but that was going to change this week. The Saddle Club was going to travel.

Kate's family owned a dude ranch called the Bar None, and Stevie, Carole, and Lisa's big Christmas present from their families was a trip out West to visit Kate for a few days before Christmas. Today was Friday. They were leaving bright and early Sunday morning. Since Christmas was on Thursday, it was going to be a quick visit. They all wanted to be with their own families for Christmas Day.

"Can you believe it?" Stevie said when Lisa and Carole were both on the telephone line. "All the way out to the ranch for three days. I can't wait!"

To some people, it might have seemed odd that the girls would travel so far for such a short visit, but Kate Devine's father was a retired Marine Corps pilot and he worked part-time flying a private plane. The best part was that the good-natured owner of the plane made frequent trips to nearby Washington, D.C. Frank Devine rarely made a trip to Washington without taking a plane full of Saddle Club members back West. This trip would be no exception.

"We haven't been there in the winter before," said

Stevie. "It's always been pretty warm weather. Since the Bar None is in the mountains, I bet it's going to be cold."

"No bet on that one," Carole said. "Frank called Dad and gave him a list of the clothes we're supposed to bring. First thing on the list is long underwear!"

"And what comes next? A second set of long underwear?" Stevie asked.

"No, it's gloves, scarves, sweaters, earmuffs, mittens, and heavy jackets. I think Dad is going to let me raid his Marine Corps foul-weather-gear closet," Carole said.

"I have things I wore skiing in Vermont," Stevie said. "Those should keep me warm enough."

"You know my mother," Lisa said. "She's already been to the mall and bought me warm but stylish clothes for the visit!"

The girls laughed. Lisa's mother was very fashion-conscious and always saw to it that Lisa's wardrobe was complete.

"Uh-oh," Stevie said. "That means Frank Devine is going to have to trade up his boss's airplane for a bigger one just to accommodate your eight suitcases, right?"

"I promise—no more than three," Lisa said.

"Right, one for each day we're there," Stevie said.

"Exactly," Lisa agreed. "Would you expect less from my mother?"

"Not for a minute," Stevie assured her. "But I bet your

5

mother had quite a time at the mall. It's just crammed with Christmas shoppers this time of year."

"Oh no," Carole said.

"What?" Lisa asked.

"Christmas shopping. Going to the Bar None means we lose four days of Christmas shopping," Carole said.

"You have *four days* of shopping to do?" Stevie asked. "I only have two days of shopping to do, but I've only got half a day of money, so that simplifies that!"

"That's not what Carole meant," Lisa said. "She means she only has one day of shopping to do, but since we'll be at the Bar None, she's losing three days to procrastinate!"

Carole laughed. "Oh, you know me too well. I guess I just got so interested in working with Starlight for the drill Max designed that I've forgotten about all the gifts I need to get."

"Does that mean you haven't even bought presents for me and Lisa yet?" Stevie asked.

"Oh, um, no. I mean, of course I got *your* presents months ago," Carole assured Stevie. "I'm talking about stuff for other people."

Lisa thought it sounded as if Carole probably hadn't gotten her a present yet. That didn't bother her. In fact, it made her feel a little better. She had gifts for her family, but she didn't know what to get for Carole and

Stevie. Now she'd been reminded that she had only one day to get something for them—and that day was going to be mostly taken up with Horse Wise.

Their Pony Club met on Saturdays at Pine Hollow. The riders had named the club Horse Wise because that was what they hoped it would help them become—wise about horses. Meetings started at nine o'clock on Saturday mornings and lasted until early afternoon. That would leave a very short time to do any more shopping. Lisa was going to have to get her mother to take her over to the mall right after Horse Wise.

"Maybe we'll get to town while we're at the Bar None," Carole said.

"It's a teeny little town," Lisa reminded her. "And besides, who wants to go into town when there's so much to do at the ranch?"

"And so little time to do it," said Stevie. "This *is* going to be a short trip."

"Then it means that we're going to have to work harder to pack all that fun into three days," Lisa said.

"There she goes again, being logical!" Stevie teased.

"Well, if I'm really going to be logical, then I'm going to have to start thinking about packing now. There won't be much time tomorrow, and on Sunday we're out of here first thing in the morning," Lisa said.

They all agreed it was the sensible thing to do.

"See you tomorrow!"

7

"Good night."

"Happy trails."

But Lisa didn't start thinking about her packing right then. First she needed to think about Christmas. She went to sleep thinking about finding the perfect Christmas presents for the two best friends in the world.

"Now, COLUMNS SPLIT and circle back at a trot!"

Stevie kept her eyes forward and sat straight in the saddle. Max wanted all the riders to go through the whole drill practice with military precision. If the movements weren't precise, then the whole thing just looked like a bunch of horses and riders milling around a ring.

Belle perked up her ears. Belle was a mixed-breed horse, part Arabian, part American Saddlebred. There were probably some other parts in there as well, and Stevie was convinced that one of them was mind reader. Belle had a way of seeming to know exactly what Stevie was about to ask her to do.

Stevie turned Belle to the left and trotted the length

of the ring, following one length behind Carole, who was leading the column of riders through the drill.

"Nice turn, Stevie, nice," said Max.

Stevie could barely keep her jaw from dropping. Max was very good at pointing out eight things a rider was doing wrong at once. He wasn't as good at talking about what a rider was doing right. She was very pleased by his praise and couldn't help smiling.

"All right now, cut across the middle . . . don't bump into one another . . . and back into a double column," Max called out.

Finally the practice was over. Max asked all the riders to line up in front of him, and he gave comments to each of them.

"Carole, you've got to keep Starlight at an even pace."

"Yes, Max," Carole said.

"Veronica, you must pay attention. If you're not paying attention, how can you expect Garnet to follow my directions?"

Veronica didn't answer. She just pursed her lips, obviously annoyed. Veronica rarely answered when someone criticized her. That was the way she was. The Saddle Club exchanged smirks while Veronica coolly stared straight ahead.

Max had dozens of other reminders for the riders. Toes in, heels down, remember to change diagonals without being told, don't forget the pattern, and maintain an even pace, *especially* when doing a crossover. Boys and girls were trying to take in everything Max was saying so that they wouldn't make the same mistakes again. Everybody wanted the demonstration to be perfect when they performed it in a couple of weeks.

Stevie waited for her list of criticisms, but they didn't come. Max had nothing bad to say about the way she'd ridden, which was extremely rare. Stevie decided she'd remember this day for a long time.

"Now, there's one other thing," Max said. His eyes rested on Stevie for a second. Maybe this day wouldn't be memorable after all, she thought. Maybe he had just saved her for last because her list of faults was much longer than everyone else's.

"It has to do with Wednesday . . . ," Max continued.

Wednesday? They didn't have class on Wednesday and no more Pony Club until next Saturday. What was Wednesday? It was the day they were getting back from the Bar None. It was Christmas Eve. It was—

"The Starlight Ride—for those of you who are new here—is our annual Christmas Eve event. It's a nighttime trail ride through the woods. We will end up at the town green, where everybody is invited to sing holiday songs and have hot cocoa and doughnuts."

The Starlight Ride was one of Stevie's favorite Pine Hollow traditions. There was something totally wonderful about riding at night. The path through the

11

woods was decorated with princess pine and lit with twinkling lanterns. It was a magical event.

"As you know, every year I select a special rider to lead the trail ride. It's an honor because it's not an easy thing to do. It takes someone with confidence and good judgment, someone who can be responsible and set an even pace for the other riders. It's also a way I have of honoring a rider who has made a lot of progress during the year."

Stevie smiled, remembering when Carole had had the honor. She had been riding a borrowed horse—one that her father, though she didn't know it, had already bought for her Christmas present. Starlight had been named for the ride. She could still see Carole with the torch in her hand, leading all of Pine Hollow through the woods. It had been a great night.

"And this year, it's clear to me that the rider I most want to honor and who will do a fine job for us is Stevie Lake."

Stevie shook her head. What was it Max had just said? It sounded like her name, but that really wasn't possible. She wasn't the kind of girl who got honored. She was the kind of girl who got sent to the principal's office. It must have been somebody whose name sounded like hers.

On either side of her, her best friends were grinning.

"Yay, Stevie!" Lisa said.

"I knew it! I just *knew* it!" Carole said. She reached over and clapped Stevie on the back.

"Me?" Stevie said.

"Of course it's you, silly," Lisa told her. "You're going to lead us all!"

"Really?" Stevie asked.

"You'll be up for it, won't you?" Max asked.

Stevie felt a grin spreading over her face. Max had chosen her to lead the Starlight Ride. She, Stevie Lake, was going to be the front rider.

"Leading this group through the woods?" she said. "Sure, it's a piece of cake. It's just like a game of Follow the Leader, right? Let's see—we can go in circles, maybe ride backward in our saddles—I guess there isn't anybody else at Pine Hollow who is better at Follow the Leader than I am—"

"Um, Stevie," Max said. He sounded as if he had become just a little dubious about his choice.

"Joke, Max. It's a joke," Stevie assured him. "I will be the best Starlight Ride leader you've ever known." Then she thought about the night Carole had led the ride. "Or at least the *second* best," she corrected herself, making everybody laugh.

"All right, then I want you all here by six o'clock to tack up. We'll have inspection at six-thirty, and the trail ride will begin at seven. It's going to be cold. Wear proper riding clothes, but also be sure to wear warm jackets and gloves."

He went through a long checklist of the things everybody should bring and the things everybody should remember. Stevie knew she should be listening, but her thoughts kept drifting. All she wanted to do was picture herself leading the Starlight Ride.

What a wonderful Christmas it was turning out to be. First the trip to the Bar None and now this. That meant Wednesday was going to be a busy day. Their plane was supposed to land back in D.C. in the middle of the afternoon. Then they'd have to drive through heavy traffic back to Virginia. They'd make it, though. For something as important as the Starlight Ride, nothing could go wrong.

"Stevie, do you have any questions?" Max asked before he dismissed the group.

"Just one," Stevie said. "Could somebody pinch me?"

Lisa and Carole were only too happy to oblige.

Max told all the riders to untack and groom their horses and ponies. The meeting was over.

Stevie, Carole, and Lisa cross tied their horses in a row so that they could chat as they untacked and groomed. Carole talked practically nonstop about how happy she was for Stevie.

"It's really a great honor, you know. We all know you've been working hard with Belle ever since you got

14

her, and now we know that Max knows it, too. What's more, he knows all the progress you've made. Just wait until he hands you that torch and you go out in front of all the other riders. It's the greatest feeling in the world. Belle's going to like it, too. She's a show-off, you know. She likes being the center of things—"

"Oh, Stevie, this is going to be so great!" Lisa said, interrupting Carole's analysis. "It's exciting."

"And mostly it's going to be fun," Stevie said.

Stevie considered that the most important part of the Starlight Ride—the fact that it was fun.

For a while the girls worked in silence. Stevie had gotten so excited about the Starlight Ride that she forgot she had to hurry now. Her father had promised to take her to the mall to shop for Lisa and Carole, if and only if she got home by three o'clock. She looked at her watch. She had twenty minutes. She brushed Belle faster.

Carole's mind was racing. She had to catch the 3:15 bus to the mall to finish her Christmas shopping. She didn't think she had much time, but she didn't want to look at her watch. She didn't want her friends to know she was in a hurry because she still had to buy them presents.

Lisa kept glancing through the dingy window of the stable to see if her mother's car was there yet. Her mother had agreed to pick her up at Pine Hollow to take her out to the mall. Finally the car pulled in. Now the

15

trick was going to be getting out to it without letting her friends know what she was up to. She didn't want them to know she was going to the mall to look for their Christmas gifts. Lisa looked at her watch. She couldn't wait any longer. She finished grooming Prancer.

"Oh boy," she said, dropping a dandy brush into Prancer's grooming bucket. "I've got to go. Mom's here. We're going to my godmother's for tea this afternoon. You guys doing anything?" she asked, trying to sound casual.

"Nothing as exciting as tea with your godmother," Carole said. "I have to catch the three-fifteen bus so I can get home and wash my hair this afternoon."

"What about you, Stevie?" Lisa asked.

"I'm going straight home. I've got some, um . . . I need to . . . well . . . ironing. I have to iron all my clothes so I can pack tonight," Stevie said.

Well, that answered that. Lisa could head for the mall without worrying about getting caught. She told her friends she'd see them in the morning, then took Prancer back to her stall and hurried out of Pine Hollow.

Her mother reached over and opened the door to their car. Lisa climbed in. She was glad her friends didn't remember that her godmother lived in Missouri.

"MEET ME BACK here in one hour, Stevie, okay?" her father said to her as they got out of the car in the mall parking lot.

Stevie looked at her watch. It was 3:35. One hour wasn't much time. She nodded and waved to her father, then ran more than walked into the first store she found.

I've got to get something perfect for Lisa and Carole, she thought. She looked around, her eyes scanning the shelves, convinced that she would see the perfect thing in an instant—or at least in less than an hour.

There was nothing on the shelves around her, and for a moment she couldn't understand why. Then it came to her: She was in a hardware store. In a way it wasn't surprising. That was the store her father was going to. He was giving himself a new power drill for Christmas. But somehow she didn't think she was going to find the perfect gift for The Saddle Club in a hardware store.

There isn't a wrench in the world good enough for my friends! Stevie declared to herself with a giggle as she headed into the main passageway of the mall.

She was systematic when it came to shopping. She took the escalator up to the top of the mall and began walking quickly down the halls to see what stores might offer possibilities for her friends.

Clothes? Her friends both had very nice clothes. Stevie looked down at her sweatshirt and jeans, which were covered with a faint dusting of horsehair and hay. She didn't think she'd be very good at selecting clothes for them.

There was a record store. Now *that* had possibilities. They all liked music. The problem was that Carole had recently developed a taste for country-and-western music and Stevie didn't share that taste. Stevie preferred rock—classic and modern. She was afraid that if she bought an album for Carole that *she* liked, Carole would hate it. But if Stevie bought something she herself hated, Carole might find out and be insulted. She decided against buying anything in the record store.

The next shop that caught her eye was the bookstore. She veered into it and, purely from habit, went straight

18

to the horse-book section, where she quickly analyzed everything on the shelf.

"Got it, got it, don't want it, Carole has it, Lisa has it, don't want it, can't afford it, Carole has it, Lisa's parents are giving it to her . . ."

There was nothing there. She checked out the paperback section and saw that the three of them were completely caught up with the most recent titles in their favorite series. She had to go to another shop.

She hurried out of the bookstore. She dashed past the scent shop, a candy store, three shoe stores, two electronics stores, a toy store, an athletic store, and a department store.

She scooted down the stairs to the lower level. She tried another bookstore, with no better luck. She glanced at the little specialty carts in the middle of the aisle. A mug for each of her friends? With their names on them? No, she didn't think so. Lisa and Carole weren't exactly coffee drinkers. Earrings with horses on them? No. The nice ones were too expensive and the cheap ones were too tacky.

She looked at her watch. Fifteen minutes gone and she hadn't spent a penny! She sighed. Why was it that Stevie had had no trouble buying presents for her three brothers (whom she often hated), but when it came to shopping for her best friends (whom she always loved), it was hard?

Maybe because it mattered so much to her that she get exactly the right thing.

Something ahead of her glinted in the sun. It was at the cart that held specialty glass items. Sometimes there were nice things. Stevie stepped forward and squinted. Was it possible? There were horses made of glass—dozens of them, all different sizes and shapes. And they were pretty. There was one with a beautiful arch in its neck, and another flipping its tail . . .

CAROLE STEPPED OFF the bus. It was a good thing the same bus that went to her house also stopped at the mall. The next one would be there in a little over an hour to take her home. That was all the time she had because she still needed to pack. Until then, she had a very important job to do. She wanted to get the nicest possible Christmas presents for her two best friends.

She'd done all her other shopping. She'd gotten her father some CDs of classic golden oldies. He loved everything about the 1950s—especially the music. She knew he was going to love the ones she was giving him this year. Also, she and her father had shopped together to buy gifts for their cousins in other parts of the country. Those had gone out in the mail weeks ago. There were things that Colonel Hanson could be Marine Corps–style efficient about. Family Christmas gifts were among them.

So now all that was left was shopping for Stevie and Lisa. But it wasn't easy to buy things for people you cared about as much as Carole cared about her best friends.

Her first stop was the bath store. There were oodles of sweet-smelling bubble baths, shower gels, and scented powders. None of them seemed like something she wanted to give to Stevie and Lisa. She decided to try someplace else.

There was an earring shop. Some of the earrings were nice, but not nice enough; and on the ones that were nice enough, the price tags made her shudder. She moved on. Next she came to the toy shop. Her friends were much too old for toys—except for model horses. Lisa collected those. There was a nice selection, but Lisa had all of them already, except for one big one, and that was too expensive. Carole hoped Lisa's parents were getting her that one for Christmas. She wondered if she should call them and tell them about it.

She headed back into the main walkway of the mall. It was crowded, but what else would she expect on the last Saturday before Christmas? She had to work her way through the masses of people to be able to see into the store windows. There was little in them to interest her. There were scarves, but Lisa and Stevie had perfectly good scarves. Another window displayed a pretty sweater that might look nice on Lisa—if Carole had $180! And there was a coat Stevie would really love for $280. Not exactly in Carole's budget.

At that moment a cloud overhead shifted and sunlight streamed into the mall hallway, sparkling brightly on something. Carole blinked and looked ahead. There was something very shiny. Was it glass? She stepped forward to take a closer look.

LISA'S FAVORITE SHOP at the mall was the tack shop. She made a beeline for it as soon as her mother dropped her off. Surely it would have something right—and by that Lisa meant perfect—for Carole and Stevie. Where better than the tack shop?

But what?

Neither of her friends actually needed tack. They both had saddles and bridles for their horses. That was a good thing, too, because tack was very expensive. Unfortunately, they also didn't need the inexpensive things she could afford. She said no to riding crops, horse shampoo, saddle soap, and polo bandages. There was a really good video on show jumping, but it was way out of her budget. There was one beautiful model horse, but she was the one who collected the models, not her friends. She hoped her parents knew about the big new model and that it would be under the tree on Christmas morning. There was, however, nothing here that she wanted to give Stevie or Carole.

22

Her next stop was the fancy candy store. There were some really tempting goodies, but she didn't like the idea of candy for her friends. It would be gone too soon (especially if she helped eat it), and then there would be nothing to remember of hers from this Christmas. No, she wanted something that would last, something that would make her friends think of her every time they used it or saw it.

She thought again about the show jumping tape. Maybe she could get an advance on her allowance. No, that wasn't practical. And she wanted to get something *now*, today.

She left the candy store and wandered through the crowd, hoping for inspiration. And then she saw it— there, ahead, on a cart in the main walkway of the mall.

"Perfect!" she said out loud, stepping forward, almost in disbelief that her wish had come true.

"Lisa?"

She stopped. She looked. It was Carole.

"I thought you were washing your hair," Lisa said.

Carole's hand flew to her head. "I, uh, I had to get some shampoo," she said.

Then another voice piped up. "Carole? What are you doing—oh, Lisa!" It was Stevie.

"What about your ironing?" Carole asked.

"My *what*? Oh, right, my *ironing*," Stevie said. She gulped. "Well, you know when you use that spray starch,

23

it just makes the ironing go so fast it seems like nothing." Stevie turned to Lisa. "And *tea* with your *godmother?*" she asked. "That was pretty quick."

"We had éclairs," Lisa said. "That's French for lightning, you know, because that's how fast you want to eat them. Mom and I cleared the platter in a matter of minutes."

Stevie glanced at her watch. "Seconds, I would say," she corrected her friend skeptically.

"Well, they were small éclairs," Lisa said, hoping to add some authenticity to the ridiculous statement she'd just made.

Lisa glanced over at the booth she'd been heading for. She didn't want Stevie and Carole to know where she'd been going or why. She had to distract them. She remembered that the Burger Pit was nearby.

"To tell you the truth, I'm still hungry," she said. "Anyone interested in ruining her appetite for dinner?"

"Always!" Stevie said enthusiastically.

"Lead the way," Carole said.

A few minutes later they were seated at a table at the Burger Pit, eating ready-made, none-too-good cheeseburgers. Stevie took a final bite and looked again at her watch.

"Listen, I just remembered one more blouse I have to iron," she said. "You guys just relax. No need for you to hurry, but I've got to get out of here. See you tomorrow morning." Before her friends could say a word, she waved a cheery good-bye, dropped her wrappings in the garbage can by the door, and headed back into the crowd.

Carole and Lisa lingered a few minutes over their fries, chatting about everything except what had brought them to the mall. They both agreed that they were eager to get out to the Bar None and would have a wonderful time with the Devines.

"And especially with Kate," Lisa added.

"And don't forget Christine," Carole said. Christine's family lived near the Bar None, and she would be bunking with the girls during their visit.

The conversation was stilted. Carole and Lisa had other things on their minds.

Carole looked at Lisa's nearly full soda cup and the half serving of fries she had left.

"I think I'd better get going," Carole said. "You don't have to hurry on my account . . . it's just that I need to . . ."

Lisa sighed. It looked as if Carole was actually leaving. She hoped so—it would give her a chance to finish her errand.

"So, well, then, I'll see you tom—" Carole started to say.

"Okay," Lisa agreed quickly. "Bye."

Finally she was gone. Now all Lisa had to do was to give Carole a good head start so she wouldn't run into her again and she could—finally—get back to the stand with the pretty glass horses. Carole and Stevie were going to *love* them!

"WELCOME TO THE Bar None!" Kate Devine called out to The Saddle Club, even before they could get their bags out of the back of the dude ranch's wagon.

They didn't bother with the bags right away. Hugs and greetings were much more important than suitcases!

Kate and her mother, Phyllis, were part of the hugs, and they were quickly joined by Christine Lonetree.

The girls were tired from their long plane ride, but the sight of the Bar None refreshed them.

"It looks so different!" Lisa said, declaring what each of them had noticed. The Bar None in the winter was totally different from the place they knew in summertime and fall. There were remnants of a snowstorm on the

27

ground, with neatly shoveled paths from the main house to the guest bunkhouses and from everywhere to the barn.

Most people thought of dude ranches only for summer vacations, but the Bar None was always open. The cattle needed to be tended every day, and the horses could be ridden year-round. There wasn't much vegetable farming to be done in the winter, but there were plenty of activities visitors could enjoy.

"Come on, now, everybody grab a suitcase—or three in Lisa's case—and let's get settled into our favorite bunkhouse," Kate said. "I've already brought my pajamas and stuff out there."

Lisa took a bag in each hand from the back of the wagon. "I was able to limit my mother's packing to two bags this time," she announced proudly.

"Good, then you'll only need two bureaus this time instead of the usual three!" Kate teased.

"Oh, just you wait," Lisa said. "You're all going to be wanting to borrow my clothes!"

"As long as they're warm," said Kate. "Because the first thing we're going to do is go for a ride. Are you up for that?"

"Definitely," Stevie assured her. "As long as the horses are."

"I warned them about you," said Kate. "I told them

you'd be riding them nonstop from the moment you got here until you left. The horses didn't seem to mind."

"Great," Carole said as they clattered into the bunkhouse. It was cozy, warm, and welcoming, with a large room that had bunk beds and a bathroom the girls would share. In the middle of the room was an old-fashioned potbellied stove. When the girls had stayed at the ranch in the summer, the stove had seemed like a quaint decoration. Now that it was the middle of winter, a much-needed coal fire glowed in it. Warmth radiated throughout the large room, supplementing the meager heat that came from clanking radiators by the windows.

"So what are we waiting for?" Carole asked.

"I thought you'd never be ready to ride!" Christine joked.

"Did someone say ride?" Stevie asked, pulling a pair of riding gloves from her jacket pocket.

"That's what I heard," Lisa said. She reached into the top of her larger suitcase and pulled out a pair of cowboy boots. She removed her snow boots, pulled on the riding boots, and said, "So let's go."

"Don't you want to change into something spiffier?" Stevie asked, looking at the two overstuffed suitcases beside Lisa.

"I don't think the horse will care," said Lisa. "And if I have to wait one more minute to get into the saddle, I'll scream."

"Then we'd better hurry," said Kate.

The five girls scurried out of their cabin and headed for the corral, where their horses were waiting for them.

There was someone else waiting for them, too: John Brightstar. He was the son of the main wrangler at the Bar None, and about a year older than the girls. While he liked all of The Saddle Club, he and Lisa were special friends.

His face lit up when he saw the group.

"Hi, there, dudes!" he said, welcoming them. Stevie, Lisa, and Carole greeted him warmly.

"I heard you were coming, so I got your horses ready," John said. The girls each had a favorite horse at the ranch. Carole rode a strawberry roan named Berry. Stevie's horse was a skewbald cutting horse named Stewball. Christine's horse, Arrow, was staying at the Bar None while she was there to visit The Saddle Club. Kate rode a gray mare named Moonglow. Lisa's choice was a friendly dark bay mare named Chocolate.

"I gave Chocolate an extra serving of mash so she'd be ready for an extraspecial ride, just like you asked," John said to Lisa.

If Stevie's eyes hadn't deceived her, she was pretty sure she'd just seen Lisa blush. And then she realized why. When John said that, it meant that Lisa had been in touch with him before they'd gotten to the Bar None, and that meant that the two of them must have been writing letters to each other. That was fine. There was no reason why they shouldn't. The curious part was that Lisa would be writing letters to a boy and not telling her two best friends about it! She and Carole exchanged quick looks. Carole had caught it, too.

"Hurry up, girls. It gets dark early these days," Kate said. "We've got some riding to do!"

John had put out all their tack, so the girls quickly saddled up their horses. Minutes later they were ready to head out.

Kate led the way, cutting a trail through the powdery snow on the meadow. It wasn't deep snow and it didn't seem to bother the horses at all. There was just enough to remind the girls that it was winter.

Carole took a deep breath, welcoming the crisp air into her lungs. They were riding on the same land they'd traveled many times during the summer. She could see the same promontories and lush meadows, only now the grass poking through the snow was cold and dry, and there was barely enough to support the Devines' livestock through the winter.

They passed the outcrop of land that lead to Parson's Rock. Carole smiled, remembering summer trips there. On their first visit to the Bar None, everybody from the ranch had made the strenuous climb to the top, where they'd had a birthday cookout for Stevie. It didn't look the same in the middle of winter.

31

"Hey, look! Horses have been on the ridge over there!" Christine said.

"Is that knowledge the result of your amazing tracking skills, inherited from your Native American forebears?" Stevie asked.

"No, I think it's the result of being able to recognize hoofprints in snow," Christine said, laughing.

Everybody looked where she was pointing. At the crest of a nearby ridge, there were clear indications of horses— a lot of horses.

"Come on, I bet the herd's over there," said Kate. "Let's see how they're doing in the snow."

The Bar None's herd varied in size, but there were generally about a hundred horses. The ranch regularly used about half the herd for their guests. Those horses were kept in corrals near the main house. The rest of the herd was allowed to roam the huge ranch, contained by the fences that marked the Devines' property lines. Every year the Devines would cut out some of the herd, selling off extra animals and saddle training others. It was a good way for the Devines to assure themselves of a constant supply of horses. It was also a way for the ranch to give its guests an astonishingly beautiful view from time to time.

The herd was always a surprise for the Saddle Club. They all spent a great deal of time around horses and believed they knew them well, but it was only when they came to the Bar None that they saw them in a totally natural state—roaming free and wild.

The girls rode to the crest of the hill and then stopped to watch.

Horses naturally form herds, which usually have a dominant stallion leading the mares, their foals, and miscellaneous geldings. The Bar None herd broke into smaller groups in the summer. In the winter, however, when food was scarce, the horses sometimes formed a single large herd that shared the meager resources. That was what the girls saw in the meadow below.

The afternoon sun had melted enough of the previous day's snow to bare the winter grass. All around the meadow, horses bowed their heads to the shoots of green, munching carefully.

One horse raised his head and sniffed at the air. Lisa knew that was because the wind had shifted. He was smelling them. He looked up at the crest of the hill, staring intently for a moment.

"He's checking us out," Lisa said, pointing to the stallion. The girls smiled because Lisa was obviously right.

In a few seconds the stallion put his head down to the grass again, clearly satisfied that the riders represented no danger to his herd. None of the other horses even looked their way.

Kate clucked her tongue and gave Moonglow a little kick. The mare obediently moved forward. All five girls rode closer to the herd. A few of the horses finally looked at them, without curiosity. Most simply continued eating.

On one side of the herd, two dun mares and a dark chestnut gelding seemed to be playing a game.

"Tag?" Carole asked.

Stevie looked more closely and shaded her eyes. One of the mares lunged at the other and then ran after the gelding when he fled, giving a small, frisky buck as she did.

"No, I think it's more like touch football," Stevie said after serious consideration.

Lisa laughed. The idea of horses playing a complicated game like touch football seemed silly, but as she watched she saw what Stevie meant. Maybe it wasn't so outrageous after all!

"And the mares are winning!" Lisa said.

"Go for it, girls!" Christine added.

"Look at that one," Carole said. She was pointing to a mare that wasn't exactly up to playing touch football right then. She was a dark chestnut with white socks on her hind legs. She had a huge belly.

"She's got to be due any day now," Carole said. "Or maybe it was last week. I don't think I've ever seen a mare so pregnant!"

The horse lumbered uncomfortably. She seemed to make an enormous effort just to move a few feet to some fresh grass.

"The herd is definitely going to be larger soon," Stevie said.

"But not a minute too soon for that mare," said Christine. "She *is* huge. I hope her delivery goes okay. But it's amazing to me how horses seem able to have their babies without much fuss out here. It's rare that we have to call the vet for a foal. I think this lady's going to figure out how to get this done on her own, too."

Christine turned Moonglow back toward the hill. "We should probably head back. It's late and we definitely want to be home before dark. It gets fiercely cold once the sun goes down."

As if nature had been listening, a cold wind swept the meadow. The girls turned their collars up and tugged their hats down against the gust. They turned their horses toward the ranch. Bundled up, they rode steadily and in silence, each remembering the remarkable sight of the herd, the playful threesome, and the pregnant mare.

"Whoa!" Kate called from the front of the line. The rest of the girls drew up to where she'd stopped.

Carole shaded her eyes to see what had stopped Kate. Two riders were coming toward them. Kate waved to the riders. They waved back.

"Must be some of our guests," she said. "But I didn't think anyone else was riding out today." She clucked her tongue, and Moonglow started walking toward the pair. Kate was ready to greet them and suggest that they ride back to the ranch together. "I wouldn't want guests to get lost on a night like this one's going to be," she said.

But as they neared the pair, Kate realized that she didn't know them and they weren't guests of the ranch. One was riding a tall gray horse and the other a bay with white socks. The horses hadn't come from the Bar None, either.

"Welcome to the Bar None," Kate said. Stevie noticed that she didn't sound very welcoming. In general, people didn't ride across other people's land without permission. It was possible they'd gotten permission from Kate's parents. Until she knew what the situation was, it was wise to remain polite but cool.

"Oh, have we left the Westerlys' property?" one of the men asked.

"Yes, you have," Kate told him. "Their land ends at that fence over there. You're on the Bar None now. It's all fenced off. How'd you get here?"

"A gate," the second man said.

"Gate?" Kate asked, raising an eyebrow.

He pointed behind him. There was no gate. There was only fence—except that the fence was broken.

"Oh dear," said Kate. "We'll have to get that repaired right away. In the meantime, you can use it to return to the Westerlys'."

Lisa admired the way Kate spoke. She continued to be

polite, but she was firm. This wasn't public land, and strangers weren't welcome without an invitation.

"Isn't there BLM rangeland over here?" the first man asked.

Lisa knew that BLM stood for the Bureau of Land Management. That was a government agency that controlled millions of acres of wild land.

"There's no BLM rangeland anywhere near here," Kate said. "Now, we've got to get back and I want to make a temporary repair of that fence. Why don't you two go back the way you came so we can fix the fence behind you?"

"Okay," the first man said, shrugging. The two of them turned around and rode back through the broken fence.

Kate watched them disappear over a hillside. "Dudes!" she said disgustedly. "They don't know the first thing. Imagine not knowing the difference between a gate and a broken fence!" She dismounted and unhooked the rope from her saddle horn, then tied it around the standing posts, fashioning a temporary fence.

"Even the greenest dude should know the difference between a broken fence and a gate," Carole agreed.

"Well, they're gone and the fence is repaired. This should hold until John and his father can get out here to repair it. In the meantime, it'll keep our herds on our land and keep Mr. Westerly's herds on his land."

She gave a final tug on the rope and, satisfied, climbed back into Moonglow's saddle.

"It's almost sunset," Kate said. "Want to watch the sun go down from Parson's Rock?"

That sounded like a wonderful idea.

"Race?"

She didn't have to ask twice.

JOHN AND WALTER Brightstar were waiting for the girls when they returned to the barn.

"It's twilight," Walter said. "You girls should have been back before now."

"We were worried," John said. He looked quickly at Lisa.

The expression on John's face answered any questions in Carole's mind about whether he was still interested in Lisa. His look showed genuine, total concern. Carole thought it was touching that he cared so much.

"We had to stop and fix a break in the fence," Kate said, conveniently forgetting to mention the side trip they had taken to watch the sunset.

"Third one this week," John said. "Must be the weather. So where was this one?"

Kate described the area to him as she and the rest of the girls dismounted and unsaddled their horses. Walter said he and John would go out first thing in the morning to make repairs.

Once the horses were taken care of, the girls returned to their bunkhouse to wash up and change for dinner. It had been a long day of traveling, by airplane and by horseback. They were tired and hungry.

"I'm not sure if I'm so tired I can't eat or so hungry I can't sleep," Stevie said.

"Oh, I bet if you put your mind to it, you'll be able to eat," Kate said to her. "Particularly when I tell you that I heard a rumor that my mom has made her special Southwest stew for dinner—the one with the hint of mesquite. And I think I saw some wild rice."

"I can always sleep later," said Stevie quickly, pulling a sweater over her head.

The girls tromped through the cold night to the main house. The bright lights inside glowed warmly, welcoming the girls before they reached the porch. When the door opened, the rich scent of Phyllis's stew wafted toward them. Stevie aimed straight for the dining room, but was sidetracked by a group of unfamiliar people.

"Kate, why don't you introduce your friends to our other guests," Frank said.

First the girls met Mr. and Mrs. Katz, who were staying in the main house. They were an older couple, perhaps in their sixties. The first thing Stevie noticed about them was that they both had really nice smiles, as if they were happy people.

"Oh, please call me Ellen," said Mrs. Katz. "I'm not used to 'Mrs. Katz' yet; I may never be."

"And I'm Fred," said Mr. Katz, offering his hand. The girls shook it. "We're on our honeymoon," he explained. "That's why Ellen isn't used to being called Mrs. Katz."

Stevie tried very hard not to look surprised. After all, there was nothing wrong with older people getting married and going on honeymoons. And what could be nicer than spending a honeymoon at the Bar None? She decided then that she liked the Katzes.

"And these are the Finnegans," said Kate. "Mr. and Mrs. Finnegan and their son, Gary."

Gary and his father stood up and shook hands while Kate finished the introductions. They were a good-looking African American family. Gary and his father were tall and slender. Mrs. Finnegan was picture-perfect. In fact, the whole family looked picture-perfect. Their clothes were expensive, and each outfit almost matched the others, blending colors and patterns. Stevie couldn't help wondering if they'd all just stepped out of a wardrobe room somewhere.

"The Finnegans are staying in the Creek Suite

bunkhouse," Kate said. The remark seemed casual, but Stevie knew it was meant to convey information. The Creek Suite was the Bar None's premier accommodation. It was a separate house, much fancier than the bunkhouse the girls were occupying. It had two bedrooms, two bathrooms, and a large sitting room with a fireplace. It also had its own den and kitchen. It meant the Finnegans were VIPs—very important people.

"Is anybody here hungry?" Phyllis asked brightly. The response was overwhelmingly enthusiastic.

One of the nice things about the Bar None was that when it wasn't too crowded, the Devines and all the guests ate together at a long table in the dining room. It made everyone feel as if they were part of one big family.

"So you girls went on a ride this afternoon?" Gary asked while platters were being passed around the table.

"That's what we came for!" Lisa said cheerfully.

"Where to?" Gary asked.

Stevie described their itinerary, explaining that they'd gone as far as the horse herd, a few miles out on the range.

"That was a pretty short ride," Gary said.

"Well, we just got here," Stevie said.

"Oh, then I guess when you get better you'll be able to take longer rides," he said smugly.

Stevie blinked, confused at first. Then she understood. Gary thought the fact that they'd just arrived meant they were greenhorns who could handle only a short ride. Stevie had an urge to say something about how he'd probably been lazing in front of the fireplace while they were loping on the snowy range. Then she remembered that the Finnegans were staying in the expensive Creek Suite. They were VIPs. This was no time for her to indulge her famous sharp tongue. Instead she smiled politely.

"We're going riding again tomorrow morning. Would you like to join us?" she asked.

"Uh, sure," Gary said. "I don't mind going out with you all."

Stevie bit her tongue. She wasn't certain whether Gary was saying it wouldn't kill him to ride with amateurs or whether he was pleased to be invited. She chose to act as if it were the latter.

"What time do you ride?" Gary asked. "About ten-thirty?"

"Well, we might be *back* by then," Stevie said, indulging herself just a little. Lisa and Christine stifled laughs.

"Actually, we go out before sunrise," Kate explained. "It's a tradition with us."

"Oh, fine," said Gary. "I myself like a long early-morning ride."

"Bareback," said Christine.

"Really?" said Gary.

43

"It's the greatest," Carole assured him. "You're going to love it."

"Well, it just happens that I've always enjoyed riding bareback," Gary said. "A well-trained horse is a joy to ride when there's no saddle to interfere. I try to ride bareback whenever I can, in fact."

"It'll be nice to have you with us," Kate said. "We usually leave about six o'clock. Will you be ready?"

"Of course," Gary said.

Stevie was glad she'd been polite to Gary. Apparently he was a good rider. It might even be fun to have him along in the morning.

"So, will you girls be here for Christmas?" Mrs. Finnegan asked, changing the subject.

"Oh, no ma'am," Carole answered. "We're leaving here on Wednesday morning. Frank will fly us back to Washington then."

"But don't worry, Mrs. Finnegan," Frank said. "I'll be back in time for the traditional Bar None Christmas."

"What's the traditional Bar None Christmas?" Kate asked. She seemed oddly surprised about her own family's Christmas traditions.

"Our tradition is to make the holiday as traditional as possible," Phyllis said, shooting her daughter a meaningful look.

"Oh, right," Kate said, as if suddenly remembering.

"It's hard to say what's traditional," Stevie remarked.

44

"It seems to me that everybody's traditions are very different from one another."

"Well, what's important to you about Christmas?" Carole asked. "I mean, aside from getting lots and lots of wonderful presents."

"Hmmm," Stevie said thoughtfully. "I think it's what we have for breakfast Christmas morning."

"What's that, Stevie?" Phyllis asked.

"Eggs Benedict," Stevie said. "I don't know why. We just always have. Every Christmas. And I've got to say, it's not Christmas without eggs Benedict. The funny part is that I don't really like eggs Benedict. I mean, I like the eggs and the muffins and the ham, but I don't actually like the hollandaise. I always scrape it off my eggs. But if I don't have the chance to scrape the sauce off my eggs, I don't feel like it's Christmas."

"Stevie, did anybody ever tell you you're weird?" Kate asked.

"Often," Stevie assured her. "So, what's everybody else's idea of Christmas?"

"My mother's stollen," said Kate, smiling at Phyllis. "That's a sweet bread from Germany. It's got wonderful things in it, like cinnamon and raisins. We have it every Christmas morning."

"I've got to have pot roast on Christmas Eve," said Lisa. "My mother makes it the best, with a rich, thick gravy. No mesquite flavor, but it's still delicious!"

45

"In my family we mingle traditional Native American Indian customs with Christmas," said Christine. "When my grandmother was alive, she always made us wait to open our presents until she told us the story of the origin of our people. She wanted us to have pride in our past as well as our present and future. After Grandmother died, my mother took on the job. We joke that the tradition in our family is 'past before presents.' "

Everybody at the table laughed. Then Ellen Katz spoke. "Well, we're newlyweds, so we don't have any traditions yet. But they won't be Christmas traditions, because we're Jewish."

"But Hanukkah's already started," Stevie said. "Do you have a menorah?"

Ellen smiled. "Yes, we do. We brought it with us. And each night after dinner, we've recited the prayers and lit the candles. Do you know about this?"

"I sure do," said Stevie. "My boyfriend's mother is Jewish, so they celebrate both holidays. I like the biblical story about the oil in the temple lasting for eight days, although Phil says I'm just jealous because he gets presents for eight days, not one! Actually, though, I like the candles."

"We light candles, too," Carole said. "But not for Christmas or Hanukkah. My father and I celebrate Kwanzaa."

"What's that?" Phyllis asked.

"It's a celebration of African cultures," said Carole. "It's not a religious holiday, but it sort of reminds African Americans where we came from. In a way, I suppose it's a little like Christine's grandmother's story. Anyway, Dad and I have a candelabra called a *kinara* that holds seven candles. Each of them represents one of the seven principals of Kwanzaa. The most important one is the black candle called *umoja*, which means unity." Carole looked over at the Finnegans. "Do you do anything for Kwanzaa?" she asked.

Mrs. Finnegan shook her head. "Oh dear, no," she said. "We're usually much too busy at this time of year to do any celebrating at all. It's just that this year, we all knew we had to take some time off."

"Time off?" Stevie asked. "From what?"

"Don't you know us?" Gary asked. "We're *the* Finnegans."

Stevie bit her tongue again. Of course she knew they were the Finnegans, she just didn't think that was so special except for the fact that they had enough money to rent the Creek—

"Of course!" Carole said. "You're the *Finnegans!*"

Stevie was about to ask Carole why on earth she and Gary were babbling such nonsense, since anybody could figure out that people named Finnegan were the Finnegans, but Carole answered the question for her.

"I have all your albums! I love your music! I sing every

song along with you—though not nearly as well, of course. Don't mind my friends. They don't know anything about country-and-western music, but I'll set them straight because, well, because you're *the Finnegans!*"

Carole's voice trailed off. She couldn't say anything else. She was simply overwhelmed.

6

As soon as the bunkhouse door shut behind the girls, they all started asking Carole questions.

"What do you mean, *the* Finnegans?" Stevie demanded.

"*The* Finnegans," Carole answered. "Don't you know *anything?*"

"Not about country-and-western music," Lisa said. "Are these guys a big deal?"

"Just the biggest, that's all," said Carole. "The last time they had an awards ceremony, the Finnegans wore a hole in the carpet going up to the podium to accept little gold statues. They're great! You don't know how lucky we are to have them here. And then there's *Gary.*"

Stevie had been wondering about him. So she asked. "What about *Gary?*"

"Well, he's their son," Carole began.

"We figured that one out," Stevie said. "But what about him?"

"He's just joined their act. I think his parents were waiting for his voice to change or something, but now he performs with them all the time. And all the reviewers say he may be the best part of the act. You should *hear* how he sings."

Lisa put her hands on her hips and regarded her friend carefully. "If I didn't know you better, Carole Hanson, I'd swear you just swooned!"

"I think I did," Carole confessed. "I know you guys don't care about certain kinds of music, but, trust me, what the Finnegans do is really great. Maybe we can talk them into performing for us."

"No way," said Kate. "They are VIP guests. If they want to do something, *they* decide to do it. We don't *ask* them to do anything."

"Oh, well," Carole said. "At least we get to ride with Gary tomorrow. That's going to have to do."

Kate stoked the fire in the stove while the girls put on their pajamas. As she changed, Stevie thought about the conversation they'd had at the dinner table.

"You know, we forgot the most important Christmas tradition of all," she said.

"What's that?" Lisa asked sleepily.

"The Starlight Ride," Stevie said. "I suppose you just wanted to ignore it because *I'm* going to lead it this year?" she teased.

Two pillows hit her simultaneously.

"What's the Starlight Ride?" Christine asked.

Lisa explained it to her. Christine and Kate thought it sounded like a tradition they ought to start at the Bar None.

"You're going to love it," Stevie assured them. She climbed into her bunk.

Normally a night in the bunkhouse meant hours of talk for The Saddle Club. Tonight, however, the time change had caught up with the Virginia girls. They were tired.

Carole pulled the covers up to her chin and closed her eyes. Time to sleep meant she'd have time to dream about the Finnegans . . . and tomorrow morning's ride . . . She was asleep before she could even think the final words of the sentence: . . . *with Gary.*

THE NEXT MORNING, Carole was the first one out of bed and dressed. She was also the first one out the door. She had a very important assignment. She'd been chosen by her friends to knock on the Finnegans' door and ask if Gary really wanted to join them on their ride.

Her hands were shaking when she raised her knuckles

to the door. She hadn't had any problem talking to Gary before she knew he was Gary *Finnegan*, so she couldn't think of a reason why she should have a problem now. Still, she did. She meant to knock only twice, but her hand was shaking so hard, she hit the door five or six times.

Gary opened it.

"Oh, I'm sorry," Carole said, blushing.

"For what?" Gary asked. "I was waiting for you to come get me."

"And here I am," she said finally. "The others have already gone to the stable. Are you ready?"

"Sure," he said, smiling at her.

Carole thought Gary Finnegan's smile was going to make her knees melt. That thought kept her from being able to say anything else until they arrived at the stable. There were six horses waiting for them. Carole was relieved to see Berry. As long as she was anywhere near a horse, she knew what she was supposed to do. She took Berry's reins from Kate and climbed onto the strawberry roan's back.

"Your horse is named Spot," Kate said, handing the reins to Gary. Carole was pleased that Kate had chosen Spot for Gary. Spot was an Appaloosa that Kate had ridden often until she got her own mare, Moonglow. Spot was an excellent horse, well trained, quick, and smart. Any rider would be happy on him.

As they set off in the cool morning twilight, the country looked different than it had the day before in its afternoon winter wear. To the left, in the east, the first hint of dawn made pink streaks in the velvet sky.

"Oh, I'd forgotten how much I love this," Lisa said. "No matter how cold it is!"

"Ha! You call this cold?" Gary asked. "Why, I remember riding through four-foot drifts of snow in Montana when it was thirty below zero. Now *that* was tough on the riders!"

"To say nothing of the horses," Lisa added. "Why were you doing that?" She thought it must have been an emergency to put the horses and riders at such a risk.

"It was pretty country," Gary said. "I didn't want to miss the view."

"If you want a view, then you're going to have to ride up to Parson's Rock later on," Kate said. She pointed at the outcropping to their left.

"What's the matter with riding up it now?" Gary asked.

"It's a steep path. It's too dark right now to do it safely, and it's too steep to do it bareback. We can ride out this afternoon and we'll show you the way."

"I don't know that I'll want to ride again today," Gary said. He tugged Spot's reins and made the Appaloosa turn to the left. "I want to go up there now."

"I really don't think we should—" Kate began.

53

"It's okay. I understand why you don't want to, but I want to do it," Gary said. "You go on ahead. I'll follow your trail in the snow."

"Gary—" Carole began. Kate cut her off.

"If you want to, go ahead. Just please be careful. My parents would never forgive me if I let anything happen to you," Kate said.

"Mine wouldn't, either," Gary said. "Don't worry. I'll be fine."

"Okay," said Kate. With that Gary spurred Spot to a trot and the two of them disappeared into the evergreen patch that covered the base of the hill capped by Parson's Rock.

"Is he going to be all right?" Carole asked.

Kate shrugged. "He says he's a good rider. He'll have to be to make that climb. But one thing I know is that if it can be done, Spot will do it. If it can't be done, Gary's going to find himself on one stubborn horse! He may or may not make it to the top. He definitely will be safe. Come on, let's get going. I think we're going to get the best view of the sunrise from the crest of that hill over there. We may even be able to find the herd again."

The riders moved forward through the high meadow. They reached the crest of the hill a moment before sunrise. The five of them waited silently for the sun to make its appearance. They didn't have to wait long. Nor could they see much when it happened.

54

It hadn't been easy to tell before the sun came up, but most of the sky was covered with a thick blanket of clouds. The sky brightened in the east as the sun came up, but it was hardly the breathtaking sight they'd seen on cloudless mornings in the summer.

"I think it's daylight," Christine remarked. It made them all laugh.

"Well, tomorrow is another day," Stevie said philosophically.

"I'm not absolutely certain about that," Kate said.

"About tomorrow being another day?" Stevie asked.

"Well, of course, it is, but look at those clouds. That's not just an overcast. Those clouds are heavy. They have a purplish cast to them. You know what that means, don't you?"

"It's going to rain grapes?" Stevie asked brightly.

"Not exactly," said Kate, laughing. "It looks to me like snow—and lots of it."

"Oh, goody! We can build a snowman!" said Lisa.

"Make angels!" Carole declared.

"Have a snowball fight!" Stevie said.

Kate shook her head sadly and looked at Christine. "I guess three girls from Virginia don't know what a real snowstorm can be," Kate said.

"Sure we do," said Carole. "We have occasional snowstorms in Virginia. We had a good inch and a half last week. They even closed school for a day!"

Christine hooted. "For an inch and a half of snow!"

"The streets were slippery," Lisa explained.

"With an inch and a half of snow!" said Kate. "Wait until you see what happens with fifteen inches of snow!"

"Fifteen?"

"Well, maybe not. But we'll see. Anyway, expect snow before the day is out. Come on, let's quit the weather report and get moving. Maybe we can find the herd." She urged Moonglow forward, toward where they'd seen the herd the day before.

On the way, Kate was pleased to see that her temporary fence was holding and would stay secure until John and his father could come out later in the morning. However, she wasn't so pleased when she saw that there was a new break in the fence.

"What the? . . . ," Kate mumbled.

"Again?" Christine said.

"How could that be?" Lisa asked.

"Maybe the winter has just been too harsh for the fence," Carole suggested.

"Maybe," said Kate. She didn't sound as if she believed it, though. Fortunately she had another rope on her saddle horn. Once again she fashioned a temporary fence with the rope and made a mental note to tell the Brightstars to look for two breaks in the fence, not just one.

Kate turned out to be right about the herd. The horses

were very near where the girls had found them the day before. They had just moved to another side of the open meadow. It was still early and most of the horses were at rest, standing with their heads lowered. A few were lying down. The stallion looked up as the riders approached but, sensing no danger, lowered his head quickly.

The girls stopped to watch. Lisa scanned the herd, looking for the dun mares and the gelding that had been playing "touch football" the day before. She didn't see them.

"Where did they go to?" she asked Stevie, who was looking for the same threesome.

"Beats me," she said. "Maybe the winners went to Disney World?"

"Very funny," Carole remarked.

"They might be around someplace," Kate said. "But the herd is a sometime thing. It's possible that some of the group broke off and went to a new place. We could find them over that hill to the left or beyond the one to the right. If this land were completely flat, it would be easy, but it's not. They are around."

Lisa was disappointed. She had felt as if the playful threesome were her new friends. She wanted to see them again.

"There's the pregnant mare!" Stevie said. It wasn't hard to find her. She was, if anything, larger than she'd been the day before.

"She looks like she's about to give birth to a three-year-old," Carole joked.

They heard hoofbeats behind them. They turned to see Gary approaching at a lope.

"He shouldn't be riding that fast on frozen ground," Stevie said to Lisa. "That's not safe."

"Especially when the ground is covered with snow so he can't see if there are rocks or anything," Lisa said. She was about to signal him to slow down, but he was already slowing Spot to a walk as he reached the party.

"Did you get to the top?" Kate asked.

"I sure did," Gary said. "And it was worth every bit of work."

"Quite a view, isn't it?" Carole said.

"You bet it is. I watched the sunrise from up there. It was glorious."

"Well, there are a lot of beautiful things around here," Carole said. "And I'll—I mean *we'll* be glad to show them all to you."

"Why, thank you," Gary said graciously.

"Right now, the most beautiful thing I can think of seeing is a stack of pancakes about fifteen feet high," Stevie said.

"I think that means it's time to get back to the ranch," Kate said. "Let's go. Carole, you lead the way."

Carole was pleased to do so. Gary rode next to her,

and the two of them were quickly chatting easily about horses and then about country-and-western music.

Lisa rode next to Kate. Stevie and Christine brought up the rear.

"That Gary is a mighty powerful person," Kate said to Lisa.

"Oh, I guess money and talent can make someone powerful," Lisa remarked.

"Even more than that," said Kate.

"What do you mean?"

"Well, at this time of year, I've never been able to see the sunrise from the top of Parson's Rock. I guess that means Gary is so powerful that he can move the sun!"

"You mean he lied about getting to the top?"

"He had to," Kate said. "In December, the sun rises to the southeast, not the east. There's no southeast view from up there."

Lisa laughed. "I guess maybe when you're rich and famous it's hard to admit you can't do something."

"Personally, I think admitting to failure is preferable to lying, but then I'm not rich and famous, am I?" Kate said.

Behind them Stevie burst into song. She often did that when riding at the Bar None, though her friends had done everything they could to convince her that even the coyotes did a better job of singing than she did. Stevie was a girl with many strengths and talents. Singing wasn't one of them.

"Oh, give me a home! Where the buffalo roam!" she screeched.

Gary turned around to look at her. Before she could take another breath, he took up the tune where she'd left it off.

" 'And the deer and the antelope play,' " he sang. His voice was everything Carole had said it was—rich and strong, velvety smooth and gentle.

"Maybe a voice like that *can* move the sun," Lisa said to Kate.

"Maybe," Kate agreed, sighing with pleasure at the joyous sound of Gary Finnegan's music.

"ARENT YOU COMING in for breakfast?" Carole asked Gary when they returned to the ranch.

"No thanks," said Gary. "I'll eat with my parents in our suite. We've got some work to do on a new arrangement after that. Since you're such a fan, I'd invite you to listen in, but my parents get funny about secrecy when we're trying something new . . ."

"Oh, you don't have to apologize," Carole said. "It just means I have something to look forward to. And when it hits the top of the charts, I'll know where it began."

"Thanks," he said. Then he veered off to the Creek Suite.

Stevie tugged at Carole's sleeve. "You're gushing, Carole."

Carole started to blush.

"Don't worry," Lisa said calmly. "I don't think he noticed."

"Oh, I hope not," said Carole. "It's just that he's—"

"I know," said Stevie. "He's Gary Finnegan."

"I guess you *do* understand," said Carole.

"I don't, but I have to say, the boy can sing," Stevie said. "In fact, he sings much better than I do."

"*Stewball* sings better than you do," Lisa teased.

"That's not my singing you're hearing. That's my grumbling stomach," Stevie said.

"There may be no cure for the voice, but there is a cure for the grumbling stomach," Kate said. "And I can smell it from out here. Let's go."

The five girls tromped into the main house. The closer they got to the dining room, the more delicious breakfast smelled. By the time they sat down, they were starving. Fortunately Phyllis had made an enormous stack of pancakes. The plate emptied quickly while the guests served themselves. As fast as Stevie could say "Pass the butter, pass the bacon, pass the syrup—uh, please," she was ready to eat.

The Katzes were at the table and asked the girls about their morning ride. The girls were delighted to reenact it. They told how they'd found the horse herd in case the Katzes wanted to ride there later in the day.

"Not too late, though," Kate said. "It looks like it's going to snow."

Frank Devine joined the others at the table. As he poured himself some coffee, he turned to his daughter.

"Do you know anything about a break in the fence?" he asked her.

"Sure do," she said. "In fact, there were two. We saw one last night and I tied it up with my rope. Then, when we were out there this morning, there was another. I might not have noticed it at all except for the two idiots who came over from the Westerlys' land yesterday. They said they'd come through the gate. Only a total greenhorn can't tell the difference between a broken fence and an open gate. Anyway, I told John and Walter about both breaks. They're going out there this morning to fix them."

"I think I'm going to have to go myself," Frank said.

"Why?" Phyllis asked him as she pulled up her own chair to the table.

"Well, I just had a call from Westerly. He told me that half his herd of horses is missing. He asked me to check and see if they somehow got onto Bar None land and joined our herd."

"They might have," Kate said. "That fence was wide open all night long."

"No, Kate," Carole said. "We saw the Bar None herd. There were no extra horses there. In fact—don't you remember? There were fewer horses than we saw yesterday."

"Fewer?" Frank Devine asked.

"Sure," Stevie told him. "We especially noticed that three horses who'd been playing touch football yesterday—"

"Touch football?" Ellen Katz said.

"Don't mind Stevie," Frank said, smiling. "She has a very active imagination."

"But she's also got sharp eyes, Dad," Kate reminded him. "We were watching a pair of dun mares and a gelding play around yesterday. They definitely weren't there this morning."

"Do you think part of the herd might have split off?" Frank asked.

"Of course. That's what I told the group, too. But when you add that to the call from Mr. Westerly . . ."

Stevie's eyes lit up. "Horse rustlers!"

"Stevie!" Carole said, trying to shush her friend. She explained to the others, as if to apologize for Stevie's well-known eccentricities, "Sometimes her imagination is *too* active. That's when she can't tell the difference between greenhorn dudes and horse thieves."

"She might be on to something," Frank said. "Westerly doesn't have anywhere near as much land as the Bar None. If he says half his herd is missing, he's been able to look everywhere. It's possible they came on over to our land, but then how do we explain the fact that some of our horses seem to be missing?"

Carole looked at her nearly empty plate thoughtfully. "There could be a number of explanations," she reasoned. "First, maybe no horses are missing. They just wandered out of sight and Mr. Westerly is too lazy to go look. Second, maybe some of his horses came onto your land and divided your herd and we only saw the remaining part. Or . . ." She paused, trying to think.

"Horse rustlers!" Stevie declared. Clearly her imagination was in high gear. Her eyes glowed with excitement. "I've seen movies about this," Stevie said. "Trust me. You've got some mighty fierce varmits out there. Why, anyone who would take a mind to steal another man's horseflesh is nothing but a low-down, rotten sidewinder." With every word she spoke, Stevie slipped more deeply into a movie-cowboy caricature. By the time she got to declaring that horse rustling was a "hangin' offense" and suggesting that they put together a posse to "give them critters what they deserve," Lisa could barely contain her giggles.

Frank Devine had a more modest proposal. "While I appreciate your loyalty and good intentions, Stevie, I think you've taken it a bit too far. We *do* have modern criminal investigation techniques available to us these days, so I don't think a 'necktie party' is quite what's called for."

"It was just an idea," Stevie said meekly.

"Yes, I know," said Frank, smiling. "But I think we need to have a better idea of what's going on before we try to—what is it they say?"

"Take the law into our own hands?" Stevie suggested.

"Right," Frank said. "Anyway, I think I'll ride out and do the fence repairs myself. That'll give me a chance to look around and make an assessment of—"

"Them dirty varmints?" Stevie offered.

"—the situation," Frank finished.

"You don't think it's anything to worry about, do you, Dad?" Kate asked.

"I think any time you've got two breaks in a fence that didn't have any breaks in it a few days ago, when your neighbor is complaining about missing horses and your own herd seems to be short, and when your daughter has seen strangers with poor excuses trespassing on your land —well, it's a good time to assess the situation."

Phyllis stood up and began clearing plates from the table.

"Be careful out there, dear," Phyllis said to Frank. "I was listening to the weather forecast this morning. They're calling for snow."

"Well, it's almost Christmas," Frank said. "Of course there'll be snow."

"Actually," Phyllis said, "they mentioned something about rather a *lot* of snow."

8

STEVIE EYED THE last pancake on the platter.

"You can't," Carole said.

"Can too," Stevie said. She was always ready for a challenge, especially when the challenge involved pancakes. She slipped the flapjack onto her plate, buttered it, smothered it with maple syrup, and dug in. Slowly. She would do almost anything rather than admit she didn't have room for just one more.

Kate appeared from the kitchen to wait for Stevie's plate.

"Maybe she'll just keep eating until lunchtime," Carole said.

"Okay by me," Kate said. "That's one less plate to

67

wash. And speaking of washing, I promised Mom I'd help her with the Christmas baking. It's part of those Christmas traditions we have that I didn't know we had until the Finnegans booked the Creek Suite. Anyway, it'll keep me busy until lunch. Do you all have plans for the morning?"

Lisa stood up from the table and pushed her chair in. "I thought I might check my tack," she said. "It might need a little cleaning."

Stevie and Carole exchanged glances. Lisa's tack was fine. Going to the barn after breakfast didn't have anything to do with tack, but it did have a lot to do with John Brightstar.

"See you later," Stevie said, excusing Lisa, who left with a little spring in her step.

"I'm out of here for a while, too," Christine said. "But nothing near as romantic as cleaning tack. I'm meeting some school friends in town. We agreed to finish our Christmas shopping together. Anybody want to come along?"

"No, I'm all done with my shopping," Carole said.

"Me too," said Stevie.

"You are?" Carole asked.

"Sure," Stevie said.

"Oh," said Carole.

"Okay, well, then I'll be back here for dinner. See you all then."

"Bye," they said.

Carole watched Stevie consume the last three bites of her pancake. She shook her head in awe. "I never thought I'd see someone eat fourteen pancakes at one meal."

"Fifteen," Stevie said. "But one of them was little."

"You beat all," Carole said.

"I always do," said Stevie, wiping her mouth fastidiously. "I'm good at pancakes, but I'm a true sharpie at Monopoly. Want to try your luck?"

"Well, sure," Carole said. "Free Parking?"

"Definitely."

The two girls headed for the game closet in the lounge. They found the Monopoly box, and it took them only a few minutes to set up the game and begin. Stevie took the old shoe. Carole was the iron.

Stevie won the toss of the dice. She threw a ten. "One, two, three—oh, Just Visiting." She moved the shoe to the space next to Jail. "Speaking of 'just visiting,' isn't it nice that Lisa gets to visit with John while we're here?"

Carole tossed the dice and ended up on Connecticut Avenue. She bought it. "I guess so," Carole said. "But sometimes it seems as if she's got a boyfriend wherever she goes."

Stevie threw the dice and landed on Community Chest. " 'Second place in a beauty contest,' " she said, accepting ten dollars from Carole, the banker. "They aren't really boyfriends," she said. "I mean, not like Phil and me."

"Maybe not," Carole said as she bought New York Avenue. "But there are an awful lot of them."

Stevie held the dice thoughtfully. "Okay, there's John," she said.

"And Enrico in England. Don't forget about him," Carole reminded her.

Enrico was an Italian boy who had come to America and whom Lisa had also seen in Italy. They'd become very close friends when The Saddle Club had traveled to England and competed against Enrico's Pony Club team in mounted games.

"Oh, yes," Stevie said, tossing the dice. "One, two, three, four—Chance." She picked up a card. She gave the bank fifteen dollars for a poor tax. "Aren't I ever going to get to buy anything?"

Carole moved to Illinois Avenue and bought it. "And don't forget about Skye," she said.

"Skye isn't a boyfriend," Stevie said. "He's a famous movie star. That doesn't make him a boyfriend." The girls had met Skye Ransom when he'd fallen off a horse in New York City, trying to learn to ride for a movie. He was the heartthrob of twenty million teenage girls in America; but to The Saddle Club he was a friend. They'd taught him to ride and saved his job in the movie.

They'd each seen him a couple of times when he'd returned to Virginia for visits. Lisa had had a very special time with him in California.

"He kissed her!" Carole said.

"It wasn't a mushy kiss—just a nice kiss," Stevie said. "Like they do in the movies." She rolled an eight and went straight to Jail.

"But it was a kiss," Carole said. She bought Marvin Gardens.

"Are you jealous?" Stevie said, putting her fifty dollars onto the center of the board. She rolled a ten and picked up her fifty dollars when she landed on Free Parking.

"No, I don't think so," Carole said as she bought North Carolina Avenue.

"But you've got Cam. He's your boyfriend, isn't he?" A five and three combination got Stevie to Luxury Tax. She shelled out seventy-five dollars.

"Oh, I don't know about that," Carole said. "Cam's a really nice guy and a good friend, but he's not a boyfriend, exactly. And he's so normal. Now, if I had a boyfriend like *Gary*. . . ." She got a seven. That took her to Boardwalk.

Then Stevie saw what this was all about. Carole didn't just like Gary because he was a great singer. She had a crush on him! Gary? The same boy who boasted mercilessly about how wonderful he was and then lied about climbing to Parson's Rock?

71

Stevie was about to mention that, but she thought better of it. What harm could come from Carole's having a crush on Gary? It was Carole's crush, after all, not Stevie's. They'd be leaving in two days. They'd never see the Finnegans again. And for a long time to come, whenever Carole heard one of the Finnegans' songs, she could think about Gary with a warm spot in her heart. It seemed pretty harmless. It even seemed sort of nice.

Stevie rolled the dice. Six. That took her to Income Tax. She put her hard-earned two hundred dollars from passing Go back into the center of the board.

Carole rolled a six, too. She bought the Reading Railroad. Stevie rolled a three and moved her shoe to Chance.

"Advance token to Boardwalk," she said. She handed Carole the fifty-dollar rent. "I don't think this is working out for me," she said.

"What do you mean?" Carole asked as she bought the Electric Company. "You're about to pass Go again. That'll get you another two hundred dollars."

"Until I land on Income Tax again." And she did just that. "So are you, like, *interested* in Gary?" Stevie asked. She was trying to sound subtle. She was also trying to keep Carole from knowing what she really thought about him.

"He's cute, isn't he?" Carole asked.

"Um, I guess so," Stevie said, searching for something

that would sound complimentary. "In a sort of country-western way."

"Yeah," said Carole.

Stevie realized then that it probably didn't matter at all *what* she said. Carole was totally starstruck by Gary Finnegan.

"He's a nice guy, Carole," Stevie assured her. "I guess he's used to having girls throw themselves at him, so I don't think you should count on getting his attention. . . ." She landed on Chance. She didn't even have to read the card. She knew exactly what it would say. *Go to Jail*.

"But he's been so *nice* to me," Carole said. "You should have seen the way he smiled when I went to get him this morning. I was so nervous and he was so nice. I thought my knees would collapse. He didn't notice at all."

While Stevie tried to roll doubles to free herself, Carole bought another railroad and two more properties.

"You know, you're right," Stevie said, thinking out loud. "Gary has been particularly nice to you. He talks to you about his music and he rode next to you all the way back this morning."

Carole picked up the deed for Ventnor. "Do you think I've got a chance?" she asked.

Stevie paid the fifty dollars to get out of Jail and threw the dice. She landed on Community Chest. "A better chance than I do of winning this game!" she said. She dropped another fifty dollars in the center of the board.

"But you didn't even look," Carole said.

"You do it for me," Stevie said.

Carole picked up the card for Stevie. "Oh dear. 'Pay Doctor's Bill, fifty dollars,' " she read.

"See, Carole, some days all the luck runs one way." Stevie handed Carole the dice.

Carole smiled to herself. She felt a nice shiver of delight. Stevie watched her best friend. She knew exactly what was on her mind, and it was pure Gary Finnegan.

Well, Carole was one of the most special people Stevie knew. Gary Finnegan would be the luckiest guy in the world if Carole fell for him.

Stevie tossed the dice. An eight took her to the B&O Railroad.

"Yippee!" Stevie shrieked.

"What are you cheering about?" Carole asked. "I own it already."

Stevie handed her fifty dollars. She sighed. "Gee, I wonder when Lisa will be back from the barn," she said.

Automatically, both she and Carole looked out the window toward the barn.

They couldn't see it. The window was white. At first

74

Stevie thought the shade was pulled down. But it was up. The window was totally white because it was snowing. Both girls ran to look out. They couldn't see a foot in front of them.

"Now *that's* snow!" Stevie said. Carole agreed.

9

"THIS IS MARSHMALLOW," John said, introducing Lisa to a
dappled brown horse.

Lisa patted the horse's neck and looked into his sweet,
dark eyes. "I get it," she said. "He's the color a marshmallow is supposed to be when it's perfectly toasted over a
campfire."

"That's right," John said, smiling warmly at Lisa. She
felt her insides melt a little bit, like a perfectly toasted
marshmallow.

As her friends had suspected, Lisa's tack was in perfect
shape. She hadn't fooled anybody, especially not herself.
She'd just wanted to spend some time in the barn with
John. He was feeding the horses that were stabled
indoors, and she was helping him.

"We usually have a few horses that need special care, ones that are lame or recovering from something. Those are the ones we house in the barn through the winter."

"What's the matter with Marshmallow?" Lisa asked.

"Nothing," John said. "He just doesn't like the cold. Every year, come winter, he practically knocks on our door for cover. Dad's an old softy when it comes to sweet-natured horses like this fellow. So we let him board here until spring."

One of the things Lisa loved about people who loved horses was the special affection they seemed to have for various horses' peculiarities.

"I sure hope he doesn't spread the word," she said. "You'd have a hundred horses knocking at your door!"

"And then we'd find a way to take care of them all," John said. Lisa knew he meant it.

Together they mucked out three stalls, gave all of the horses grain and fresh hay, and tidied up the tack room. Lisa decided that the only thing nicer than doing something for a horse was doing it with a friend like John.

When they'd finished with the indoor horses, Lisa and John hefted a couple of bales of hay out to the horses in the corral near the barn. They clipped the wires and broke the hay into flakes so the horses could feed easily.

There was a nip in the air, colder even than it had been during the morning ride. A brisk wind cut across the meadows and seemed to go right through Lisa's warm, fashionable jacket.

"Oh, it's nasty out here today," she said.

John stood up and looked at the sky. "It's going to get worse, too," he said. "Snow's coming."

Lisa looked at the clouds. They were low and threatening. They seemed to be heavy with moisture, ready to burst. John was right. Snow was coming. It was just a matter of time.

"What about the herd?" Lisa asked. "What do they do when there's a big snowstorm?"

"They usually find some protection. Often we'll locate the herd huddled by a hillside, away from the wind. They paw at the snow to find grass for feed. They make out, but that doesn't mean they couldn't use a hand. Want to give them one?"

"Of course," Lisa said. "What do we do?"

"Well, we put a dozen bales of hay in the pickup truck and we go look for the herd. You saw them earlier today, didn't you?"

"Yes," Lisa said. "They were past Parson's Rock, to the east."

"Can you show me the way?"

"Of course. Can you drive?"

"Of course," John said. "I mean, I'm not old enough to have a driver's license, but out here in ranch country it's common for kids like me to learn to drive early so we can

78

drive the ranch equipment and be helpful. Dad taught me to drive when I was twelve, before I could reach the pedals easily. I'm not allowed to drive on roads where it's easy. I can only drive on the Bar None. Frank tested me himself. He says I'm as good as he is and he allows me to drive everywhere on the property. Why don't you let Phyllis know where we're going so nobody will worry about us? I'll tell my dad, and then I'll meet you out back in five minutes."

Five minutes later the two of them were piling bales of hay into the back of the truck.

"What's that?" Lisa asked, pointing to a folded-up piece of nylon.

"That's the lean-to we're going to put up to protect the hay from the snow. It won't keep it perfectly safe, but if we get it in the right direction, it will at least guarantee that no matter how much it snows, the horses will be able to find the feed we've left for them. Ready?"

She smiled and nodded. It seemed like an adventure to be going off across the high meadows in a pickup truck with her friend John. It wasn't just an adventure, though. It was also a rescue mission. They were doing something for the horses.

John slid in behind the wheel of the pickup and turned the ignition key, and the engine sparked to life, coughing against the cold air outside. He shifted into gear and eased the truck forward. Lisa couldn't believe how grown up she felt, riding high in the cab of a truck, next to John Brightstar. It was a nice truck, clean and comfortable. There was a toolbox behind the seat, a radio, and, Lisa noticed with amusement, a compass. It was hard to think that they could get lost enough on the Bar None's land to need one. It struck her as rather quaint.

When they reached Parson's Rock, Lisa told John to bear left. He turned as she directed, but she realized he hadn't needed her direction. He could see the hoofprints from their early-morning ride.

"Who got turned around?" he asked, pointing to a set of prints that led to Parson's Rock.

"Oh, that was Gary," she explained. "He wanted to climb Parson's Rock before dawn."

"He's a fool," John said.

"Just what I thought," said Lisa. "He told us he made it to the top and he said he'd watched the sun rise from there. But Kate says you can't see the sun rise from there in the winter."

"Kate's right," John said. "And you shouldn't ask your horse to climb a steep trail when you're riding bareback and it's still dark."

"He's sort of a dude, isn't he?" Lisa asked.

"Oh, you never know about the people who come here," John said. "That couple, Mr. and Mrs. Katz—I kind of thought they were dudes, but then it turned out they are both extremely experienced riders. They've

both been riding for years. They know what they're doing. You can't judge riders by how they look or what they
say, or even how long they've been riding. I've seen some
excellent beginners who just—I don't know—they *get* it.
I've also seen people who have been riding for years who
never learned a darn thing. What it comes down to is,
the only reliable way you can judge riders is by how they
ride."

"Gary rides pretty well," Lisa said, recalling his style.
"Maybe he's better than we think."

"And maybe he's just good at pretending," John said.

"Look! There they are!" Lisa said, pointing straight
ahead. The herd had shifted its position only slightly
from where they'd been at dawn. They'd moved closer to
the hill. It was as if they knew bad weather was coming
and they wanted shelter from the storm.

"Do they actually know what direction the snow will
come from?" Lisa asked, looking up at the sky to see if
she could tell.

"Probably," John said. "I try not to make the mistake
of underestimating a horse's instincts. Here. This is
where we can put up the lean-to."

He drew the pickup to a halt and climbed down out of
the cab. The first thing out of the back was the tent
material. It was a simple enough structure, barely more
than a single sheet to protect the herd's emergency feed.

81

Lisa and John worked together to pound in the stakes and secure the nylon.

"This isn't exactly a weathertight shelter," Lisa said.

"Doesn't have to be," John said, tossing his mallet and the extra rope into the back of the pickup. "It just has to keep a small area more or less free from snow."

At that moment, as if John's words had invited it, the snow began. In Lisa's experience, snow started slowly. At first just a few flakes would fall, then, within fifteen or twenty minutes, there might be noticeable flakes drifting down from the sky. After half an hour, even the casual observer would see that it was snowing.

That wasn't the case this time. The first flake of snow was accompanied by fifty million exactly like it. One moment it wasn't snowing. The next it was snowing hard. Lisa looked up and across the meadow. She could see the herd of horses lifting their heads to the snow and then turning away. Here a tail flicked. There a horse shook his head. They drew toward one another. And then Lisa realized she couldn't see them all. A few of them were completely lost from sight in the blur of snow.

"We'd better hurry," John said.

They pulled the bales out of the back of the truck, snapped the wires, and broke the bales into flakes. They worked together efficiently and were done within a few minutes. When Lisa climbed back into the cab of the truck, she was surprised to see that she was covered with snow. She brushed it off and turned up the heater.

John slid into the seat next to her and shifted the truck into gear. There was a haste to the way he did it that startled Lisa. She realized that he was hurrying because he was afraid.

"Is this a whiteout?" she asked.

"Not yet," John said ominously. He flicked on the headlights and wipers and turned the truck around. Lisa squinted through the blur that was the world beyond the windshield. All the landmarks had disappeared in whiteness. She could no longer see horses, trees, or outcroppings of rocks. She couldn't even see which part of the sky the sun was in. She could barely make out the tracks on the ground in front of them that the truck had laid not fifteen minutes earlier on the way out. That would be how they would find their way home—as long as they weren't filled in by new snow.

Suddenly the truck tracks veered to the right. They had come to the point where they'd turned by Parson's Rock. John followed the track. As he turned, Lisa noticed the compass on the dashboard shifting positions. They were now going due north. She knew it was a straight path to the Bar None. It was a comforting feeling, and then Lisa remembered how she'd been amused by the compass only half an hour earlier. She'd learned a lot in half an hour.

John held the steering wheel tightly and stared straight ahead. Every once in a while there would be an ever-so-slight break in the sea of white and he could find a landmark. He talked as if to himself.

"Yes . . . there's that tree. And the rut. Where's the rut? Do you see? . . . There it is."

Lisa stared at the blur. She couldn't help, and that frustrated her. Then there was a small flash of light behind them. She saw it in the side mirror outside her window. It was a white light, so it couldn't be their own taillights, but she didn't see it again. It was gone. She lowered her window, listening. For a brief instant she thought she heard a horse. She called out. No answer.

She shook her head, trying to clear her ears. Nothing. Nobody was there. The light had been her imagination. After all, who could be out in a storm like this?

They drove on, inching forward at a rate slower than a walk. There was an intimate silence between them. It was as if the world had suddenly become immeasurably smaller. Nothing seemed to exist beyond the three feet that they could see in front of the truck; and when they passed that three feet, there was another three feet—an endless progression of tiny little worlds. Lisa watched the compass. North, it said. They were going home.

Something moved in the white darkness in front of them. John stopped the truck and peered ahead. It moved again. There was a swishing; then it disappeared.

John waited. Then a large, dark figure came into the truck's lights. It was a horse with a rider. The swishing had been the horse's tail flicking nervously.

John rolled down his window. "Hello!" he called into the dim whiteness.

"John, is that you?" It was Frank Devine. He rode to the truck's window and peered in. "Lisa?" She nodded.

"Wow! Are you okay?" John asked Frank.

"Now that you're here, I am," Frank said. "Hold up a bit, let me come in with you."

Frank rode to the back of the truck and used his rope to make a lead for the horse. He tied it to the back of the pickup. In short order he slid into the seat next to Lisa.

"In all my years, I've never seen a storm come up that fast," he said.

"It's a good thing we spotted you," Lisa said. "I think two people could be five feet apart in this and never see each other. You know, I think I saw your flashlight a few minutes ago. I should have said something then."

"Not me," Frank said. "I'm not carrying a flashlight."

Lisa thought that was odd, but she knew that the constant motion of the flakes could have made her think she'd seen a light. At least they had Frank warm and safe with them now. They were together. They'd find their way back to the ranch.

"Do you know where you're going?" Frank asked.

"North," said John. "We took some hay out to the

horse herd and the storm came up as we were headed back. We knew we were on the right path when we got to Parson's Rock. We made the turn and I checked the direction right before the road totally disappeared. Since then I've been following as straight a line as I could, due north. I think we're about a half mile away from the Bar None."

"Sounds about right to me," Frank said. "I thought I was going north, too, and you came up behind me. Let's just hope that two great minds won't be wrong."

John looked at the compass for reassurance and began proceeding again, very slowly. When he was satisfied with the truck's speed and direction, he spoke.

"Excuse me, sir, but what on earth were you doing out here by yourself in this storm?"

"I didn't come out in the storm, John, any more than you two did. I came out to mend the fence and examine the problem myself. I thought I'd be home in plenty of time before the storm began. But I had something of a surprise."

"You mean the snow?" Lisa asked.

"Well, I guess I mean I had two surprises. I took a look at the breaks in the fence. They weren't accidents. Somebody used a saw and a pair of wire clippers on our fence."

"Why would somebody do that?" Lisa asked.

"I intend to find out," Frank said. "As soon as we get home."

"I'm trying, sir," John assured him.

Lisa blinked. A huge, dark shape loomed directly ahead. She couldn't make it out, she just knew it was there. And then she knew what it was.

"The barn!" she declared.

John stopped the truck.

"Whew," he said.

They were safe.

"Lisa!" Carole and Stevie welcomed her into the main lodge with open arms.

"You're okay!"

"I am. I'm just fine," Lisa said. "John did a great job. It was an instrument landing."

John and Frank Devine followed Lisa inside. The three of them brushed snow off their jackets. They'd accumulated a significant dusting of it in the fifteen feet from the truck to the lodge's front porch.

"What's an instrument landing?" Stevie asked, looking puzzled.

"That's what they call it when the pilot can't see the airport. He or she just does everything by what the instruments say," Carole explained.

"And the compass was my only instrument," John explained.

"Wow!" Stevie said, genuinely impressed.

"My mother just said something about hot chocolate," Kate announced. "Any takers?"

Everybody's hand went up except John's.

"I'm going to go check in with my dad and let him know I'm okay. Then I'll unsaddle Frank's horse and give him an extra ration of hot mash. He's earned it. *Then* I'll have my hot chocolate."

John nodded to the Devines and their guests. He told Lisa he hoped he'd see her later and gave her a shy smile. She told him she hoped so too and, once again, thanked him for the great job he'd done getting her and Frank back to the Bar None.

Stevie, Carole, and Kate missed none of this. Stevie even thought she could see a glow of pleasure on Lisa's face. Maybe it was just red cheeks from the cold, though.

Phyllis appeared with a tray of steaming mugs. Ellen Katz was right behind her with a bowl of marshmallows. Each of the girls took two marshmallows and dropped them onto the hot chocolate. Lisa held her mug with both hands, enjoying the warmth radiating from it. It was nice to be safe and warm back at the Bar None. She and John had had a close call out in the snow—closer than she wanted to think about.

While she waited for the cocoa to cool a bit, she

looked out the window. It was a whiteout. She knew there was a tree right outside that window, not four feet away. She couldn't see it. It was lost in the snow, just as she had been.

"So, tell us what happened," Stevie urged. When Lisa was done telling the tale, everybody was doubly glad that they'd all gotten back safely.

The living room in the lodge was old with high ceilings. A blazing fire in the fireplace warmed up the huge room and made it cozy. Flames licked at the logs and sparked upward, making everyone forget the miserable weather outside the sturdy walls of the lodge.

The Katzes were playing bridge. The four girls started playing a raucous game of Monopoly. Frank worked on a crossword puzzle, and Phyllis sat at the desk, planning meals and shopping for the next week at the ranch.

Every once in a while Frank would poke at the fire or toss on another log. The room was cheerful, buzzing with the chatter among the players and the snapping and popping of logs in the fire.

"Three spades."

"You can't buy Oriental. I already own it, and that'll be six dollars please."

"You already own everything."

"Three no-trump."

When noon came, Phyllis served up big bowls of

steaming soup and a selection of sandwiches. The girls took their lunches back to the Monopoly board.

By midafternoon Carole had amassed an enviable fortune and was getting richer and richer by the moment because nobody could safely run her gauntlet on the fourth side of the board.

"I give up," Lisa declared.

"Me too," said Stevie.

"Then I'm ready to pop some popcorn," said Carole. Her friends looked at her. "For the tree," she explained. One entire corner of the lodge's main room was taken up by a tall spruce tree that was still bare.

"We always try to make popcorn chains for our trees, too," said Stevie. "Except my brothers eat the popcorn."

"Just your brothers?" Kate asked.

"Well, Mom and Dad, too," Stevie said. "And every once in a while I have some."

"We make chains out of colored paper," said Lisa.

"And we make chains out of popcorn and cranberries," Kate said. "So what are we waiting for?"

The four girls went into the lodge kitchen, already filled with tempting smells from the morning's baking and the huge vat of stew that would be dinner. Stevie declared herself in charge of popping popcorn. Kate located the bags of cranberries. It didn't take long before the irresistible scent of fresh popcorn joined the other delicious smells in the kitchen. Phyllis produced needles and thread, and the four girls sat in a circle on the floor around the bowls, ready to create "the most spectacular decorations ever put on a tree," as Stevie had pronounced they would be. It seemed like the perfect activity for a wintry afternoon three days before Christmas.

The lodge door opened wide, bringing in a gust of wind and a brushing of snow.

"Hello!" called the three Finnegans.

"You made it okay from your cabin?" Phyllis asked, standing up to greet them.

"The snow seems to be letting up now," Mrs. Finnegan said. "There's a lot of it and plenty of it is blowing around, but not so much is falling down."

"Well, come on in and get warm by the fire," Phyllis said. "The girls are making chains for the tree—"

"And we need two more for bridge," said Ellen Katz. "Would you like to play some more?"

"Sure," said Gary's parents. They joined the Katzes at the card table.

Frank Devine looked out the window and then opened the door to check on the weather. It was still snowing, but it didn't seem to be a blizzard anymore, just a gentle snow. Lisa peered through the window. The whole world was fresh, clean, and white. It looked so beautiful and serene, it was hard to imagine that only a few hours ago it had been dangerously fierce.

There was a loud noise then, approaching the lodge.

"It's the snowplow," Frank said. "They've cleared the main road and our drive is open."

"That's always nice," said Phyllis. "Even when we have no intention of going out, it's good to know we can."

"Actually, I do have an intention of going out," Frank said. "I want to get to town to talk to the sheriff about the breaks in my fence and the missing horses from my herd and Westerly's. Something's up and I think the local law needs to know."

A look of concern crossed Phyllis's face. "The weather's so unpredictable. Can't you do this by phone?" she asked.

"I think it'll be better in person," Frank said. "I talked to Westerly earlier. He wants to go with me. I'll take our truck. I promise I'll drive carefully."

"In these conditions, I don't think you've got any choice," Phyllis said. "We'll see you later."

He bundled up, gave Phyllis a kiss, and ducked out the door, pulling his hat down over his ears.

"Let's see if we can't finish the tree before he gets back," Kate said. "That'll be a nice welcome."

The Saddle Club agreed.

Carole was making a pattern of two cranberries and three popcorns, then two cranberries and so on. She liked the look of the contrasting colors.

"Nice," said Gary.

"Thanks," Carole said without pausing in her work. "Would you like to try?"

"Sure," he said, sitting down on the floor next to her. She put her own strand down for a minute and found a needle and some thread. She handed them to Gary. He looked mystified.

"Would you like me to thread it for you?" she asked. Gary nodded a little bashfully. Carole pulled a length of thread off the spool.

Stevie made a strangled sound in her throat. Lisa knew exactly what it was. Stevie was thinking what a wimp Gary was! He couldn't even thread his own needle! And was that really Carole Hanson doing it for him? Lisa glared at Stevie. The Finnegans were in the VIP Suite and they couldn't be rude to important guests. Stevie saw Lisa's look and swallowed her snort.

"Here, now you knot it like this and then it'll hold. Just poke the needle through the berry," Carole was murmuring to Gary.

She demonstrated her technique, giving Gary an extra warning about being careful not to break the fragile popcorn. Lisa gave Stevie a dirty look, just in case. Stevie bit her lip.

"Ouch!" Gary cried.

"Oh, sorry. I forgot to tell you not to hold your finger on the other side of the berry," Carole said solicitously. "Are you okay?"

"What's the matter, Gary?" Mrs. Finnegan asked from across the room.

"It's my finger," he said. "I pricked it with a needle."

"Did you hurt yourself?" his mother asked. There was a great deal of concern in her voice, much more concern than any of the girls—even Carole—thought a needle prick warranted.

He examined it. Lisa could see a tiny drop of blood where he'd pierced his skin.

"I think I'm okay," he said.

"What are you doing with a needle?" Mr. Finnegan asked sharply.

"Making decorations," Gary said. "Or at least I *was*."

"You can't use a needle, Gary," Mrs. Finnegan said.

"Sure he can," Carole said. "He was doing a pretty good job of it, too, until he stuck himself."

"No, I mean you *may* not use a needle," said Mrs. Finnegan. "It's too dangerous."

Dangerous? What was dangerous about a needle? Lisa wondered. Did Gary have some rare disease or something?

"Your guitar-playing is much too important to risk for the sake of some tree decoration!" Mrs. Finnegan declared.

Lisa could barely believe her ears. And some people thought *her* parents were too protective! She couldn't wait to hear what Gary was going to say to his mother about that! His response turned out to be as surprising as his mother's reaction.

"I'm sorry. I just wasn't thinking, Mom," he said. And he put down the needle.

What surprised Lisa even more was Carole's reaction to the whole thing.

"Oh, Gary!" she gushed. "I should have known better. I'm sorry, Mrs. Finnegan. It was my fault. I just forgot to show him how to hold the berry, and then—"

"It's okay, Carole," Gary said. "No harm done. My finger will be good as new in no time, and besides, where I hurt it won't affect my playing anyway."

"Sure?"

"I'm sure," he said.

Carole spoke up again then. "Just to be sure, Gary, would you mind trying out your guitar, like in here? Would you sing for us?"

"What a great idea," Gary said enthusiastically. "How about a few Christmas carols? Would you like that?"

The look on Carole's face answered the question. Gary went for his guitar. He returned in a few minutes and sat on a chair near the girls and not far from the bridge players. He began by strumming a few chords, and then he started singing.

His first choice was "O, Holy Night." It had always been one of Lisa's favorite Christmas songs. It was both haunting and dramatic. The guitar accompaniment gave it a new and interesting quality, and she enjoyed listening. But there was something odd about the whole thing. The song seemed too big for the room and Lisa was never for a second unaware of the fact that Gary was performing. The song was a showcase for his voice, and the overall effect was a little embarrassing.

Lisa glanced at Carole. She appeared totally mesmerized. Lisa wondered how Carole could *not* be feeling some of the same discomfort.

Gary was unable to join a group and string cranberries on a thread, but he was totally able to make himself the center of attention. Phyllis Devine had put aside her work to listen. The bridge players put down their cards to listen. Even the popcorn-and-cranberry stringers were compelled to listen. Everything was centered on Gary. What had been a genial, comfortable, warm evening by the fire for everyone became the Gary Finnegan Show.

He finished singing then. There was a moment of silence, and then Carole began applauding vigorously. Everybody else joined her. Gary smiled. Actually, Lisa thought, correcting the observation, Gary *glowed*.

When the applause stopped, Gary started singing "Oh, Come, All Ye Faithful" and invited others to join in on the chorus—as if they couldn't possibly sing the verses with him. Or, Lisa thought, so that they wouldn't interfere with his solos on the verses.

Gary's parents joined him on the second verse, singing

a tight harmony with a country twang. They seemed just as happy as he to be in the limelight. They were all happy. That was when Lisa realized that whatever else might be going on—and she suspected that a great deal was—she and her friends had oddly succeeded in making the Finnegans very happy. They were VIP guests and they should do whatever they wanted.

Carole was so smart! All she'd been doing was saying exactly the right thing to make them feel welcome. Lisa wondered how she'd missed the obvious for so long.

IT WAS ALMOST ten o'clock when the last strains of "Silent Night" echoed through the Bar None lodge. Lisa looked out the window. The ground was covered by loads of fresh snow, but there was only a dusting coming down from the sky. Where there had so recently been gale-force winds, there was only a cold breeze. A few stars were visible through the broken clouds above.

"I think I'd like to check on the horses in the barn," Lisa said. "I'd like to know they're all snug."

Her friends looked at one another. Lisa cared about the horses, all right, but she wasn't any more worried about them than she had been about her tack that morning. She wanted to see John.

"Take some carrots from the refrigerator," Phyllis suggested.

"Okay," Lisa agreed.

"Can I come along?" Gary asked.

"You—wha—uh . . ." Lisa's mind raced. Then she realized there was only one answer. "Of course. But don't forget to bundle up. It's *cold* out there."

It wasn't an easy walk to the barn. Fifteen inches of snow had fallen, but the wind had redistributed it, so while some places only had an inch or two, the snow had drifted to three or four feet in others. It was Lisa's second adventurous trip of the day.

They slipped into the barn. Lisa was hoping to find a light on. More important, she was hoping to find John Brightstar there.

No such luck. The stable was dark except for the soft glow of the emergency exit lights. The bunkhouse where John and his father lived was completely dark. She was stuck with Gary.

She handed him a bunch of carrots and began introducing him to the horses. He seemed completely at ease with the animals. Lisa remembered what John had said about judging dudes by their riding skills, not by what they claimed they could do. Gary did seem to know a thing or two about horses.

"Do you get much chance to ride?" she asked him.

"As much as I can," he said. "I really love it, but our

100

schedule doesn't permit it daily the way I'd like. I was raised in horse country, you know. When my parents were on the road, making a name for themselves, I was at home on the ranch with my grandfather, learning everything I could about horses. I've ridden since before I could walk."

"Really?" Lisa asked.

"Definitely," Gary said. "Grandpa took me to my first rodeo when I was three."

"Wow, that's young to sit for such a long show," Lisa said.

"No, I mean I *performed* in my first rodeo when I was three. They had a junior barrel race. Once I'd learned how to do that, Grandpa taught me about roping and cutting. It took me a while to get good enough to compete in those, but by the time I was eight, I was the county champion."

"Eight?" Lisa had some trouble believing that. Roping and cutting were hard-learned skills that required a great deal of strength. It was difficult to imagine an eight-year-old doing them well. She kept her doubts to herself. If Carole could be diplomatic, she could too.

"I've got a whole shelf of rodeo awards. Two shelves, in fact, but those are just the ones I display."

"Wow," Lisa said with as much sincerity as she could muster. Humility was not a problem for Gary. He didn't have any.

101

"Mom's going to make me put some of them away, though. The display case was actually built for my platinum records, and they do take up more space than the roping and cutting awards."

"Wow," said Lisa. She knew she was repeating herself, but it was the most neutral thing she could say and a whole lot better than what she wanted to say. Gary and his parents were important to the Devines' business. Lisa would hold her tongue, even if that meant it got sore from teethmarks.

She patted Marshmallow and gave him a carrot. Lisa would have been glad to tell Gary how Marshmallow always came in for the winter, but he was talking about something else. She focused in on it.

". . . and she seems to be a really accomplished horsewoman. I mean, with a few more years of practice, she might think of doing some competing. . . ."

Lisa grimaced. Who *was* he talking about? She'd lost track. She had to make him continue talking until she could catch up.

"Wow," she said.

"No, I mean it. I think Carole's got some potential as a rider. . . ."

Some potential? Carole was a fantastic rider! She was the best rider at Pine Hollow and she and Starlight had won Reserve Champion at Briarwood—not to mention the blue ribbon she'd won on Long Island last summer. *Some* potential? Just who did this guy think he was?

"But tell me, uh, Lisa, do you know Carole pretty well?"

There was a change in Gary's voice, and Lisa gave him a suspicious glance.

"Sure," Lisa said. "We're best friends. Stevie and Carole and I hang out together all the time. Why?"

"Well, she seems pretty nice," Gary said.

"Very," said Lisa, wondering briefly when Gary had stopped thinking about himself long enough to notice that someone else was nice.

"I mean, I know she likes our music and all, but she seems like a special person, too," said Gary.

Gary *liked* Carole! The thought came to Lisa so suddenly that she was totally unprepared for it.

"Wow," she said involuntarily.

"Yeah, I thought so," said Gary.

The boastful, boring, Mr. Center of Attention Gary Finnegan had a crush on Lisa's best friend, and, she realized, he'd come out to the barn with her just to pump her about Carole! Lisa was truly torn. She had an opportunity here to save Carole from a lot of grief and unwanted attention. Her mind raced. She could tell Gary that Carole was pretty nice and that most people barely noticed her bad breath or that she never changed her clothes. No. Carole was her friend and she couldn't ruin her reputation at the same time as she was saving her. Friends wouldn't do that. This called for some subtlety.

"Does she have a lot of friends?" Gary asked.

Lisa thought for a moment. Everybody liked Carole. She was a nice, honest, good person. She was friendly and respectful to all. But she had two friends who were closer than anyone.

"A lot of people like her," Lisa said. "Stevie and I are her best friends—unless you want to count horses. Any horse is her best friend, especially a certain one named Starlight."

"No, I mean really close friends," Gary said.

Lisa thought that was an odd question. She and Stevie were Carole's best friends. She'd made that clear. What could Gary be talking about? *Oh,* Lisa thought. She could be so dumb sometimes! Gary was asking about *boy*friends.

"Like, ones she sees a lot," Gary persisted.

"I suppose you mean like Cam," Lisa said, letting the name slip easily.

"Cam? Is that a boy or a girl?" Gary asked.

"A boy, of course," Lisa said.

"Like her boyfriend?" Gary asked.

She was on to something here. By telling Gary about Cam and perhaps exaggerating ever so slightly, she could get Gary out of Carole's hair without making Carole look bad. Cam was a friend of Carole's. They shared a passion

104

for horses, and it sometimes seemed that they each liked horses better than they liked each other. Still, Cam would do as a boyfriend in a pinch, and this was definitely a pinch. Lisa proceeded cautiously.

"I'm not sure 'boyfriend' is quite the right way to describe him," Lisa said.

"It's more casual than that?" Gary asked.

"Not exactly," Lisa said. "I meant that it seems to me to be more serious than that." Well, she told herself, they were both *very* serious—about horses.

"I kind of thought Carole was interested in me. Did she say anything to you?"

"She loves your music, you know," Lisa said. "Stevie and I just don't know much about country-and-western music. Carole shares a passion for it with the man closest to her . . ."

She hoped Gary would think she meant Cam. Of course she was referring to Carole's father.

"Tell me about Cam," Gary said. "Is he a big guy?"

"Oh, very," Lisa said truthfully. Cam was already almost six feet tall. "He's as tall as can be—and what an athlete!" She meant he was a great rider, but she hoped she was giving the impression that he was a football player or, better yet, a wrestler or boxer.

"Quick?"

"Extremely!" Lisa said.

"But he's in Virginia, right?" Gary asked.

"Sure, but you never know with Cam. He's so crazy about Carole, he could just show up anyplace, anytime."

"Really?" Gary was beginning to sound nervous. Lisa suppressed a smile, thinking how proud Stevie would be of the job she was doing on Carole's behalf.

They were interrupted by the ringing of a telephone. It startled them both. Marshmallow's ears flicked. Lisa jumped.

The phone was right behind her on a pillar in the barn. Without thinking, she picked it up. Before she could say "Hello?" she realized that she was on an extension phone. She heard Phyllis Devine answer the call from the main lodge. The call wasn't for Lisa, and she knew right away that she shouldn't have picked up the phone, but there she was.

"Hi, hon. It's me," a male voice said to Phyllis on the other extension.

It was Frank. Lisa knew she should hang up, but if she did it now, both Phyllis and Frank would know she'd been listening. A little embarrassed, she continued listening.

"I'm at the sheriff's office," he said. "Westerly's here, and so are a lot of the other ranchers. We're not the only ones with broken fences. We're all going out together early tomorrow to look into the situation. The storm's supposed to come back later, so the sheriff has suggested we all stay here—he's got some empty beds. I'll call you

106

tomorrow if I've got any news and I'll be back by dinner for sure."

"What's this all about, Frank? Thieves?" Phyllis asked.

"I'm afraid it looks like the Butchers," he said.

"Oh dear. That's what I was afraid of," Phyllis said. "Well, you've got to do something, that's for sure. We're all fine here. I don't think I'll say anything to our guests. I don't want to alarm them. I'll see you tomorrow."

They said good night and hung up. Lisa hung up the phone after them.

"What was that?" Gary asked.

"Wrong number," said Lisa. Eavesdropping was bad enough. She certainly wasn't going to tell Gary what she'd heard. "Come on, the storm's starting up again. Let's get back to the lodge."

Gary zipped up his jacket. The two of them went back out into the night and over to the lodge, bracing themselves against the harsh wind.

Christine had returned to the Bar None when the snow had let up. When Lisa and Gary came in, she was helping Carole, Stevie, and Kate hang their cranberry-popcorn strands on the tree. The evening was drawing to a close. The bridge players had put away their cards, and Phyllis was picking up glasses and mugs. The ranch's guests were yawning and stretching, all preparing to go to bed.

"Tomorrow at dawn?" Christine asked.

107

"Definitely," the girls said.

"No matter what the weather is," Stevie said.

"Don't forget to wake me up," Gary said. "Will you knock on my door, Kate?"

"Uh, sure," Kate agreed.

Lisa smiled. Gary wasn't going to bother Carole anymore. Then she saw a look of concern flick across Carole's face. Suddenly Lisa wasn't so sure of herself.

"WHAT WAS THAT all about?" Carole asked Kate as soon as the bunkhouse door closed behind the four girls. "Why did he want *you* to wake him up tomorrow?"

"Why not?" Kate answered.

"Well, he seemed to like it well enough when I did it this morning," Carole said. "Did I do something wrong?"

"What's the difference?" Lisa asked, a little uncomfortably. She sat down on her bunk.

"That's what I want to know. Earlier today I was having the nicest time with Gary. He sat next to me at dinner. He played the guitar when I asked him. This morning we chatted all the way home on the ride. Then, suddenly, this evening he stops talking to me altogether.

In fact, he was kind of ignoring me. The only thing he said was something about not wanting my boyfriend to get the wrong idea about us. What on earth could he have been talking about? What boyfriend?"

"Cam?" Lisa suggested.

"Cam's not exactly a boyfriend," Carole said. "I mean, I like him and all, but anyway he's a million miles from here—"

"And he can't play the guitar," Stevie teased.

"Maybe he can. I don't know. But it isn't like I can't like two guys at once. So, who said anything about Cam to Gary?"

The girls looked at one another. Gary had been with the whole group except for the time he and Lisa were in the stable together.

"Lisa?" Carole asked accusingly.

"I—I guess I might have mentioned Cam when we were together," she stammered. "I don't remember *exactly*, though."

"Lisa!" Carole said. "Why would you do that?"

"He sort of asked me, you know. So I sort of told him."

Stevie sat down on her bunk and looked at Lisa in astonishment. Then it came to her. Carole had been confiding in her alone that morning when she'd confessed to her crush on Gary. Lisa didn't know. Lisa had no way of knowing. In fact, Lisa probably felt the same way about Gary as Stevie did, and she didn't know that

110

wasn't the way Carole felt at all. She thought she was helping Carole. Carole wasn't going to see it that way.

Stevie was right. Carole didn't see it that way.

"You just wanted to ruin it for me!" she blurted out. "Oh, it's all fine and dandy if Lisa has a boyfriend everywhere in the world, but the minute Carole's interested in a boy, it's not okay—especially if he's richer, more famous, and more handsome even than Skye Ransom!"

Lisa was so astonished by the outburst that she didn't know what to say. She stammered, "C-Carole, I didn't mean—I mean, I *never*—I don't know what to say."

Carole looked as if she had more to say, but then she stopped. She picked up her toothbrush and strode into the bathroom, slamming the door behind her.

Lisa was stunned. Carole really liked Gary. Why hadn't she believed that? She hadn't believed it because it was totally illogical. But there was something else more important coming through here, a true realization. It didn't matter whether Carole liked Gary or not. It was Carole's job to decide what to tell Gary, not Lisa's.

Lisa felt rotten. She felt low. She felt miserable. There was an empty pit in her stomach and a pain in her heart. She'd hurt her very best friend. She should have known better.

The bathroom door opened.

"Carole, I'm sorry," Lisa began.

"Forget about it," Carole said. "It wasn't going to work anyway."

"But I—"

"I said forget it."

Lisa stopped apologizing. However, she thought it would be a very long time before she actually forgot about what had happened.

For a few minutes a silence hung in the room. Then Stevie came to the rescue.

"So, how were the horses this evening? Everybody warm and cozy?"

"Yes," Lisa told the group. "And glad for the carrots, too. Marshmallow especially."

"Good, I'm glad to know the horses are all safe," Kate said.

That was when Lisa remembered the phone conversation she'd overheard. She'd been reluctant to share it with Gary, but she could certainly confess to her friends that she'd heard something she shouldn't have. She told them about picking up the phone.

"Your dad said something about the Butchers. Who are they?" Lisa asked. "Another country-western singing group?"

Stevie laughed a little. Kate didn't.

"He said he thought it was the butchers?"

"The Butcher family gang?" Stevie asked.

"No, I don't think that's what he meant," Kate said. "Usually when people are talking about horses and butchers, they mean something else."

The reality hit The Saddle Club then. "You mean there could be a group stealing horses in order to serve them up?" Stevie asked, wide-eyed.

"It happens sometimes," Kate said. The reality was that in some parts of the world, people ate horsemeat and considered it a delicacy.

"Oh no!" Lisa said, suddenly remembering the two dun mares and the gelding playing in the high meadow.

"It can't happen!" said Carole.

"We've got to stop them!" said Stevie.

"We?" asked Kate.

"Your dad will do what he can and that's all fine and good, but he and his friends are in town and we're right here."

"More important, we're the ones who know who's behind this," said Lisa.

"What?" Kate asked.

"Those two guys you thought were dudes," Lisa said. "Remember how even you couldn't believe somebody was dumb enough to mistake a broken fence for a gate? Well, they didn't make that mistake. They broke the fence in order to make it a gate—for the horses they'd stolen from the Westerly ranch."

"Oh no," Kate said. "Of course you're right. We've actually *talked* to these guys. We can identify them. But they're probably miles from here by now. That was yesterday afternoon when we saw them."

"No, I don't think they've gone very far," Lisa said.

"What makes you say that?" Stevie asked.

"Because I think I saw one of them, or maybe both of them, in the snowstorm this morning. I saw a light. I thought it was Frank, but he told me he wasn't carrying a flashlight. I definitely saw a flashlight. And I called out to help the person. Nobody answered. The only reason somebody wouldn't answer a call like that in a storm like we had this morning is if that person had no business being where they were: on Bar None property. Those guys aren't far away. And if they're still nearby, so are the horses."

"Now I know for sure we've got to do something," Stevie said. "We have to call your dad back, Kate, and tell him what we know. Then we've got to take action. Saddle Club action!"

"But what?" Kate asked.

"That's the part I don't know for sure," Stevie said. "I'll think of something, though. I always do. In the meantime, our ride tomorrow morning is really important. We've got to get out of here as early as possible, no matter what the weather is. There are horses to save, and we're the ones to rescue them!"

"What about Gary?" Carole asked. "I didn't think he was a really good rider. Will he get in the way?"

Carole's observation surprised Lisa. When she thought about it, though, maybe it wasn't so surprising. It would be hard to imagine Carole being so lovestruck that she wouldn't notice someone's riding skills. Lisa saw an opportunity to do some good where before she'd done only harm. She took it.

"He may be a better rider than we think," she said.

"Really?" Kate asked. Lisa did not miss the surprise in her voice.

"Well, he told me he could ride before he could walk. He won his first rodeo competition when he was three, and he's got more rodeo trophies for cutting and roping than he does platinum records."

"He's only got one platinum record," said Carole, who would, of course, *know*.

"Well, then he has at least two rodeo trophies. That's more than I can say," said Lisa.

"Then it's settled. He should come along," said Stevie.

Kate set the alarm clock. "We'll leave before dawn," she said, pulling on a jacket and boots. "I'm going to go call Dad."

"We shouldn't ride bareback," Carole suggested after Kate left.

That made sense. This wasn't a pleasure ride. This was

serious business. The lives of many horses could be on the line.

A minute later Kate reappeared. Her face looked grim.

"What's the matter?" asked Stevie.

"The phone's dead. The storm must have knocked it out," Kate answered. "It looks like we're on our own."

ON TUESDAY MORNING the girls rose in the darkness. They dressed quickly and quietly, intent on getting to work. Carole and Lisa seemed to be ignoring each other. It was easier not to talk at all.

They left the bunkhouse. Kate headed for the Creek Suite to get Gary and fill him in on the day's plan. The others went directly to the corral. Nobody had asked John to have the horses ready, so they rounded them up and saddled them themselves. By the time Kate and Gary arrived, the work was almost finished. Lisa tugged the cinch on Spot's saddle one notch tighter and then handed the reins to Gary. Everybody mounted up. Stevie brought out the lariats and gave one to each of the riders.

"What's this?" Gary asked her.

"It's a lariat," Stevie said automatically.

"What's it for?"

"To lasso stray horses," she said. He took the rope and hung it on his saddle horn as the girls did. It wasn't until Stevie was in her saddle that she thought it odd to have to explain the purpose of a lariat to someone who allegedly had two shelves full of rodeo prizes. She kept the thought to herself.

"Let's go," Kate said.

They were off. Kate led the way. The air was clear. There was no more snow falling, but in the dim light of dawn, the riders could see a now-familiar ominous cast to the morning sky. All around them the earth was covered with the fruits of yesterday's storm. It was a pure, sleek, brushed white. The wind had pushed the snow into drifts, so it was easy for the riders to make their way where the snow was shallow. If they went into the drifts, the horses' hooves splashed white snow in front of them. Kate wanted to make things easier for the horses. She stuck to the places where the snow wasn't too deep.

"This way!" Kate said, picking a path around a particularly deep drift. The others followed her.

It wasn't hard to figure out where they should start looking. They had to find the main herd and look for signs that some of the horses had left—or been taken. They passed Parson's Rock and turned toward the meadow where the herd had been for the last few days. More important, it was the meadow where Lisa and John had left protected food for them. The horses were almost certainly still in that area.

Kate was still in the lead. Carole and Christine were right behind her. Then came Lisa, followed by Gary and finally Stevie. Lisa could hear Spot's hoofs clumping and even squeaking in the snow behind her. In the midst of such a pleasant and peaceful setting, it was almost hard to remember the serious mission they had set for themselves.

Kate drew Moonglow to a halt at the crest of a ridge. Carole and Christine drew up next to her. Lisa, Gary, and Stevie joined them as they reached the top.

"There they are," Kate said. The herd was huddled in the meadow below. Most of them had their heads lowered while they rested. A few had wandered over to the little lean-to and were taking advantage of the remaining hay John and Lisa had brought out. It was a peaceful winter scene, except for one thing. The herd was only half the size it had been the first time they'd seen it.

There was still no sign of the playful trio of the dun mares and the gelding. And there was no indication that part of the herd had broken off voluntarily, because if that had happened, they surely would have returned for the food John and Lisa had put out.

"Something is definitely wrong here," Carole said.

"And we're going to figure out what it is and fix it," Stevie said.

"Let's go down there and look around," Lisa said. "Though that'll be hard because we don't know what we're looking for, do we?"

"We're going to know it when we see it," said Stevie.

One of the things Stevie's friends liked about her was that she was always certain she'd find a way to solve problems—even when she wasn't certain what the problems were.

The riders walked their horses slowly toward what was left of the herd. They didn't want to frighten the horses and scatter them into the rugged countryside. They also didn't want to make it harder to find clues by creating a profusion of hoofprints in the snow.

Lisa went over to the lean-to. She wanted to see how it had fared in the storm and find out how much hay was left. If more snow was coming, John might need to bring out more hay.

She dismounted when she got to the lean-to. Two horses were there, munching hay. Chocolate joined them. There was plenty of hay left, enough even if more snow came today. The lean-to had kept the hay mostly dry. Some of the hay was so far back in the little tent that it might be hard for the horses to reach it. Lisa pulled the remaining bales forward and broke them into flakes.

The world around her seemed to be a mixture of gleaming white outside and light brown under the protection of the lean-to. But then something gleaming white inside the lean-to caught Lisa's attention. Three things, actually. Lisa crouched down and looked. There, at her feet, were three cigarette butts. Lisa shook her head. Some people didn't care at all about the welfare of horses! What kind of a creep would leave a disgusting cigarette butt where a horse might mistake it for wholesome food? Automatically Lisa picked up the butts and slipped them into her pocket. She'd throw them away later where no horse could get them.

Lisa remounted Chocolate and joined her friends standing at the edge of the herd.

"Twenty-three horses," Kate said as she finished counting the animals around her. "I know the herd was larger than that yesterday."

"I would have said fifty," Carole said. "It's hard to tell because without all this snow on the ground, they were more spread out, but definitely there were more than these twenty-three."

"At least the mare is still here," Stevie observed, pointing to the heavily pregnant mare, which lumbered awkwardly toward a small patch of grass. "Boy, is she going to be relieved when that foal makes its appearance," Stevie said.

The riders sat on their horses and looked around.

121

"What do we do now?" Christine asked, posing the question they'd all been asking themselves.

"We follow the trail," Gary said.

"What trail? Where?" Stevie asked him.

"Over there," he said. "It's clear as can be. The trail leads up out of the meadow, headed north."

"Those prints lead into hilly, treacherous country," Kate said. "Look at the mountain beyond." She pointed to the rocky terrain which would make it almost impossible to ride one horse, much less move an entire herd.

"Well, I don't know about that, but I definitely see a trail of hoofprints. That's where you're going to find your missing herd," Gary declared.

"But it looks like prints from just a couple of horses," Christine said.

"No, that's not just a couple of horses," Gary said. "That's at least a dozen—maybe two dozen. And a few of the horses have riders, too."

"What makes you say that?" Carole asked, looking carefully at the marks in the snow.

"Well, if you know anything about tracking, then you can tell the difference between a horse with and one without a rider," Gary said. It took a minute before Carole realized that he hadn't really answered her question, but perhaps he just didn't want to share his secrets.

"You've had experience tracking?" Lisa asked.

"Of course I have," Gary said. "I spent all my early

122

years on a ranch, like I told you. I could track a horse across a mountain range with my eyes closed!" He spoke so positively that it was impossible not to believe him.

"Let's do it, then," Kate said. "You take the lead, Gary."

"Follow me, girls," he said. "I'll teach you a thing or two about tracking." He and Spot proceeded. Stevie and Christine exchanged glances and shrugged. Gary could be boastful, and he was probably exaggerating his skills, but they had to go one way or another, so why not give Gary a chance?

Lisa went after him; then came Kate and Carole, then Christine and Stevie. Lisa watched Gary carefully and paid attention to everything he did. She hoped she could learn something about tracking techniques. It wasn't an easy skill, even in snow. It was easy enough to follow the trail when the snow was deep, but there were large patches where the wind had blown the snow away from the rocky terrain and there were no hoofprints at all.

"This way, girls," Gary called. "The herd went this way."

The girls couldn't see anything. They were impressed by Gary's tracking skills because they couldn't see the invisible clues he was following.

"We'll find the herd over the next hill," he promised them. "The tracks are fresh now."

Tracks? They didn't see any tracks. All they saw was

frozen ground and rocks. The riders proceeded cautiously, allowing the horses to set a slow pace over the slippery terrain.

With each step the territory seemed to rise into the sky. Even in their warm clothes, the girls could feel that it was colder as they climbed the mountain. They had all fallen silent, knowing that each step was more treacherous for the horses than the last.

"Just ahead," Gary said. "I think I can hear them, too."

Lisa slipped her hood off to listen for the familiar sounds of horses. The only horses she heard were the ones she and her friends were riding. Gary was definitely surprising her and the others. He seemed to have very keen eyesight, and now his hearing was simply extraordinary. Maybe that wasn't so surprising. It was logical that a musician would have particularly sensitive hearing.

Finally the riders reached a huge open expanse completely covered with a foot of fresh, untouched snow. There was not a horse in sight.

Five girls looked at Gary Finnegan. He shrugged. "I must have made a mistake," he said. "They must have made a turn somewhere that I didn't notice, but I'm sure they're near here."

Kate swallowed. There were a lot of things she wanted

to say to Gary right then, but she reminded herself that Gary was a VIP guest.

"That's probably it," she said. "Maybe we should go back to where the herd is and start again."

"Maybe," Lisa, Stevie, and Christine agreed.

Carole turned Berry around to follow Kate back down the mountain. "Come on, Gary," she said. "We can check to see where the tracks veer off on our way down."

He and Spot followed Carole, who followed the other girls.

Up at the front of the line, Kate grumbled to Stevie and Lisa.

"That little side trip cost us two hours," she said between her teeth. "An hour up and now it'll take an hour back."

"It may have cost the missing herd more than that," said Stevie ominously. "Time is something they don't have."

Lisa felt a shiver run up her spine. It wasn't the cold. It was fear for what might have happened to the herd while Gary had taken them all on a wild-goose chase.

THE SUN WAS high in the clouded sky by the time the six young riders reached the diminished herd. The morning was more than half over. The girls were hungry and cold. People at the ranch might be worrying about them. Worst of all, they were not one inch closer to finding the missing horses.

Kate stood up in her stirrups to survey the land, looking for a clue they might have missed.

Gary did the same.

"I hope he doesn't tell us he found another trail," Stevie whispered to Christine. "I don't know about you, but I'm not going anywhere with him again."

"Me neither," Christine said. "I could forgive him for

126

making a mistake. What I can't forgive is the fact that all the way back, he kept saying something about how we should all keep our eyes peeled for the trail of hoofprints because that would show where we had gone wrong. And he never once apologized for leading us astray."

"Where we went wrong was bringing him along in the first place," Stevie whispered.

"Look!" Kate said, pointing across the meadow. All the riders followed her gaze to a small dip at the far end of the meadow.

"It might not be anything, but it might be the silhouette of some hoofprints. I'll go look."

"We'll come with you," Lisa volunteered.

"They didn't go that way," Gary said. "I know it. They went the way I showed you."

"You're probably right," Kate said. "But we should eliminate all the other possibilities." She nudged Moonglow's belly, and the horse started across the meadow. Gary followed close behind.

"If this ranch thing doesn't work out for Kate, she could have a nice future in the diplomatic corps," Stevie remarked to Christine as they followed the pair to the other side.

Kate's eyesight turned out to be better than Gary's. Her logic was better, too.

"I should have thought of this," she said when they reached their destination. They were on top of a rise, looking over a hilly area that led down and to the southeast. There were dozens of hoofprints all over the place.

"Why should you have thought of this?" Carole asked.

"The railroad," Kate said. "There's an old spur of tracks down there along the riverbed. It leads to the main north-south tracks. The thieves might be planning to put the horses on railroad cars. It's possible that they're following the spur to get to the main tracks. Anyway, I'm sure this is the way now. What do you think, Gary?"

It was clear to the girls that Kate was asking Gary's opinion to give him a way to redeem himself from the miserable mistake he'd made earlier.

"I don't think so," Gary said. "I'm sure they went off that way, to the northeast, the way I showed you."

Stevie rolled her eyes. "Look! There's a shoe!" she said. She was pointing to one of the prints in the snow.

"Big deal," Gary said.

"It is, actually," said Christine, trying to be as diplomatic as Kate but not quite succeeding. "See, the horses in the herd don't have any shoes on them. They are running free on the land and don't need shoes. Only a horse who is being ridden regularly will be shod."

"Oh," said Gary.

That was the smartest thing he'd said in a while, Stevie thought.

"Let's go," Kate said. She took the lead, following the trail through the fresh snow. It wasn't difficult, but it was a long ride. It made the loss of two hours on Gary's wild-goose chase all the more painful.

They rode steadily and quickly, taking much of the open land at a trot when the snowdrifts permitted it. Lisa found herself thinking that it was strange to be on such a serious mission on such an incredibly beautiful day. The sky above was still dark and the clouds were heavy, but the land around them was simply breathtaking, with snow-covered mountain peaks stretching into the distance.

"Kate! Hold up!" Gary called half an hour later. Kate drew Moonglow to a halt. She turned around and gave him a questioning look.

"There's something wrong with my saddle," he said. "It's very uncomfortable. I don't know if I can go on. I'm sure someone made a mistake tacking up this horse this morning."

Kate looked at the saddle. "No mistake," she said. "That's Spot's regular saddle. I can't think what's wrong with it or why it should be uncomfortable. Would you rather change horses?"

"No, I don't think so," Gary said quickly.

"Well, then, perhaps you'd prefer to go back?"

"Back where?" he asked.

129

"To the ranch," Kate said patiently. "Unless you have something else in mind."

"No. Not really. I was just wondering if it makes sense to go on ahead now. I mean, there could be, like, horse thieves up ahead."

"If we don't go now, there could be something worse than horse thieves—like no horse thieves and no horses!" Stevie said. "Come on, let's get going."

Kate nudged Moonglow into a trot. Gary followed, but he was scowling. Lisa glanced over at Carole. She wanted to know what her friend was thinking. Carole's face revealed nothing.

Finally, sometime later, when the sun was near fully overhead, Kate held her hand up and the other riders drew up to her.

"The railroad spur starts right over there," she said. "Just on the other side of that hill."

"So let's go," Stevie said.

"Um, wait a minute," Christine said, injecting a note of caution. "As soon as we get to the top of the hill, we'll be visible for miles. If there are horse thieves there, they're going to spot us. These guys have risked a lot to steal a herd of horses. They might not be too particular about risking something else—like us, for instance."

The words fell heavily. Lisa glanced at Gary. He gulped visibly.

"Um, shouldn't we, like, go for help?" he asked.

130

"We *are* help," Stevie said.

"But . . ."

Lisa had a few things she wanted to say, but she swallowed them. She'd decided some time earlier that morning that her life would be easier if she never spoke to Gary again.

It was Kate who made the logical suggestion. "Yes, going for help is a good idea. Why don't you do it, Gary? You were ready to go back a while ago. This would be a good time, too. You can go let my dad know where we are. He'll know exactly what you mean if you tell him we're at the railroad spur. He and the sheriff can reach this area by car or helicopter pretty quickly. Go ahead."

"Go where?" he asked.

"Back to the ranch," Kate said.

"But how?"

"Follow the trail back," Carole said to him. Those were the first words she'd spoken to him or anyone for a long time. She said them as if she were speaking to a five-year-old—and a dull one at that. Lisa felt a weight lift from her shoulders. Carole had seen the light about Gary.

He looked over his shoulder uncertainly. He clearly did not want to make the long trip all by himself. "I guess I'd better stay with you girls. You need my help," he said finally.

Each of the girls thought they would have been a lot

131

better off if they hadn't had any help from him so far. Each of them kept that thought to herself.

Stevie suggested that it would make sense for one of them to crawl up to the top of the hill and look over. It would be harder for the casual observer to spot one young person on her stomach (nobody missed Stevie's use of *her*) than to spot six riders on horseback. Stevie volunteered.

She wasn't surprised when everybody agreed that she was the best choice. When it came to doing tricky things, Stevie was always everybody's first choice. She dismounted and handed Stewball's reins to Kate. Kate pulled a set of field glasses out of her saddlebag and wordlessly handed them down to Stevie.

"I'll be back," Stevie announced solemnly, sounding like an odd combination of General MacArthur and Arnold Schwarzenegger. She saluted her friends and turned to her task.

The hill wasn't particularly high, but a lot of snow had accumulated there. Stevie trudged through the drifts, breathing hard as she neared the top of the hill. She dropped to her knees and began crawling, hoping to be invisible to anyone looking up from below.

When she reached the top, she lifted her head up over a high drift of snow and peered down into the valley.

It took her a minute to take in everything she was seeing. She was looking across a long narrow valley, formed by the creek that ran through it. Stevie knew that creek. She and her friends had crossed it many times in the summer. The last time they'd been to the Bar None, their parents had gotten caught in it during a flash flood. Now there was no water in it—or if there was, it was all ice and completely covered with snow.

Parallel to the creek bed was the bed of the railroad track that Kate had said would be there. Next to the track was a small shack. It didn't look occupied. What was occupied, however, was the large corral next to the shack. It was completely packed with horses—so packed that the horses were having trouble moving.

It angered Stevie to think of them being jammed in there so tightly. Two horses were tied up outside the corral. Stevie squinted. She thought they might be the horses those men were riding on Sunday when they'd claimed to have come through the "gate" from the Westerly land. She put the field glasses to her eyes. The two horses were a tall gray and a bay with white socks. Pay dirt!

But where were the riders? And could she be sure that the horses in the corral were stolen?

Stevie refocused the field glasses onto the corral and studied the milling horses. She wasn't absolutely certain what she was looking for—until she saw two dun mares. They were the same ones the girls had seen with the herd on Sunday. There was no lawful reason why they should be in a corral by a railroad spur miles and miles from the Bar None's land. Stevie squinted into the field glasses and fine-tuned the focus. She could see the Bar None brand on the flanks of a few of the horses. She could see a fancy "W" on another horse's flank.

"Westerly," she whispered to herself.

She knew what she was looking at. She was looking at horse thievery.

But where were the men? She scanned the property. She could see tire tracks leading from the shack to a road that wound out of the valley. Next to the shed was a bare patch on the ground. A pickup must have been parked there during the snowstorm.

It was time to report. Stevie scrambled down the hill as fast as she could.

"They're there!" she said.

"The thieves?" Gary asked.

"No, the horses. All of them. There are about fifty of them crammed into one little corral. The horses those two guys were riding on Sunday are there, too, outside the corral. But the guys aren't there. I think they had a car and they've gone into town or something. I'll tell you one thing. That corral is as full as it could possibly be. Whatever those men are up to, they've got all the horses they can steal. Sure as anything, they're going to move them out of here soon. We don't have a second to waste."

"To do what?" asked Gary, who had paled visibly during Stevie's breathless report.

Stevie blinked at him. "Why, to steal them back!"

STEVIE TOOK STEWBALL'S reins from Kate and climbed into her saddle.

"Let's go!" she declared.

"Whoa, whoa," said Kate. "Shouldn't we have a plan or something?"

"But we do," Stevie said. Only Stevie Lake could have made such a declaration. It was typical for her to have a plan in mind and just assume that everybody else had thought of exactly the same one.

"Why don't you tell us what it is?" Kate asked patiently.

"Sure," said Stevie. "First we ride down to the corral. Next we open up the gate. Then I go in on Stewball, the best cutting and herding horse west of the Hudson River. We'll shoo all the horses out into the open, and the rest of you guys herd them up this hill and back to Bar None land."

Lisa always got nervous when Stevie's plans were this simple and straightforward. "What about the thieves?" she asked.

"How could I forget?" Stevie responded. "Naturally, we have to take their horses, too. They've gone somewhere in a pickup truck or a Jeep or something, but the only way they'll be able to follow us is by horse because the terrain is so rough. All we have to do is be sure they don't have horses to do that with."

It *was* simple. The Saddle Club girls looked at one another. Nobody looked at Gary.

"Why not?" Christine asked, shrugging. They all nodded in agreement.

"Yiii-haaaaa!" Stevie called out, spurring Stewball to action.

The riders began the trek up the side of the hill as fast as they could safely go.

Lisa felt exhilarated. They were actually doing battle against horse thieves. Stevie's enthusiasm was contagious. Even Chocolate seemed to feel it. His head bobbed up and down as he clambered up the hillside. He took a deep breath at the top of the hill and began trotting down into the valley, lifting his legs high as he kicked up snow. It was as if the horses knew that they were on a rescue mission.

Carole's jaw dropped when she saw the fifty horses crammed into the little corral. *How could they do that?* she thought. She despised any cruelty to animals, but most especially horses, and this definitely qualified as cruelty. She wouldn't even let herself think about what the thieves had planned for the horses in the near future.

Berry snorted and shook his head. His gait became surer and faster and he whinnied to the horses in the corral.

The riders didn't need speak to one another. It was clear exactly what had to be done. Kate and Lisa stationed themselves by the gate of the corral. Carole and Christine waited farther away, creating a sort of chute for the horses once they were released. Gary, for once, did the right thing. He went to the far side of the corral so that he could help Stevie shoo out the horses from the outside.

Stevie opened the gate. It turned out that the horses didn't have to be told to escape. They were eager to get out of their cramped quarters. The minute the gate opened, a flood of horses burst out of the corral. Kate, Lisa, Carole, and Christine were ready for them.

The girls all had some experience at herding cattle. Horses, they found, were something else. The horses were frightened from being cooped up. They fled, and they didn't all flee in the same direction.

Stevie watched the horses racing out of the corral in front of her. She chased the last of them out of their prison and then paused long enough to unhitch the gray and the bay with white feet. She gave each a tap on the flank, and they took off with the rest of the horses.

Most of them did just what they were supposed to do. They went up the bank of the hill, headed toward home and safety. Six, however, didn't get the idea. They took off down the valley. Deep snow sprayed up in front of them as they galloped. It was a magnificent sight, but it was a route that was going to get them, and everybody else, into a lot of trouble.

As she watched the horses, something else caught Stevie's eye. She stood up on her stirrups to be sure she was seeing correctly. Unfortunately, she was. Coming along the valley by the road parallel to the creek, was a pickup—just the same size as the bare patch next to the cabin. Stevie didn't stop to figure the odds. She just knew: It was the horse thieves. They were still far away—too far to see what was going on, but they were moving fast. Stevie figured she had less than three minutes to get the strays up over the crest of the hill before the day turned nasty.

"Come on, Gary!" she said. "Help me! We've got to get the strays!"

Stevie didn't even bother to look over her shoulder to see if Gary was following her. She knew what she had to do, and she was riding the best cutting and herding horse in the world.

Stevie never understood the instincts that drove Stewball, but she knew she could rely on him absolutely. She gave him a kick and aimed him toward the fleeing strays. It was all the explanation the horse needed.

For each elegant stride the strays took, Stewball took two. Stevie held on for dear life, wondering where this horse got his energy. Snow flew up around her in clouds, exploding upward each time Stewball took stride.

Without any signal from Stevie, Stewball figured that what he had to do was get to the right of the horses and force them off to the left. That would take them uphill and to safety, even if it meant they'd still have a long ride to join up with the others.

The horse in the lead of the strays was a stallion. That meant that the mares who were trailing him would go wherever he went. *Good news, bad news*, Stevie thought. Good news if the stallion could be convinced to go where Stewball was telling him. Bad news if he had an independent streak.

Stewball drew up to the stallion and pressed forward and to the left, trying to push him up the hill. The stallion did have a streak of independence.

In the distance, Stevie could see the pickup approaching. Soon they'd know something was up. Stevie had to do something.

She grabbed the lariat off the horn of her saddle, loosened the noose, and began swinging it in the air. Soon it was making big, lazy circles.

Stevie had learned to lasso cattle on her first trip to the Bar None. She *could* do it—as long as her horse wasn't moving and the steer was standing still. Trying to rope a galloping stallion from the saddle of a galloping gelding was another thing altogether.

She took aim, crossed her fingers, closed her eyes, and let the rope fly. It arced through the cold winter air. Almost as if in slow motion, the noose shimmered and wobbled across the expanse. Stevie opened her eyes, held her breath and watched. The lopsided noose tumbled awkwardly downward and landed in the snow. She'd missed the stallion by more than ten feet!

But the movement of the snaking, flying rope had startled the stallion, and he instinctively shied from it. He ran straight up the hill and over the crest into the meadow beyond. The mares followed him obediently.

It wasn't exactly what Stevie had had in mind, but it worked. Stevie and Stewball chased them up the hill.

As soon as they were over the top the herd and their rescuers were out of immediate danger. The returning horse thieves might know where they'd gone, but without their own horses they were powerless to stop them. To be on the safe side, The Saddle Club kept the stolen horses moving toward home at a fast clip for another fifteen minutes. By then Stevie and her group of six runaways had rejoined the rest of the herd. The horses were ready to stop galloping and cantering. They welcomed a comfortable walk.

"Nice work!" Kate said to the group.

"We're wonderful!" Stevie announced unashamedly. She leaned down and gave Stewball a pat on the neck.

"Most of us, anyway," said Christine. "And speaking of him, where's Gary? I thought he was with you, Stevie."

"I thought he was, too," she said. She drew Stewball to a halt and then turned to look over her shoulder.

Someone was visible on the horizon behind her. She shaded her eyes. It was Gary. He was waving to them.

They all stopped and waited for him to catch up. He arrived breathless a few minutes later.

"I thought you'd want to know," he said. "That truck. It wasn't the guys."

"Thanks for telling us," Kate said.

"They just kept on driving right past the cabin. They didn't even slow down," Gary said.

"Then let's get these horses out of here and hope that darkness—or another load of snow—will hide their trail before the men get back," Carole said. She nudged Berry into action. The other riders followed and soon the herd of horses was moving again—on its way to home and safety.

Now that they were on their way back to the ranch, the ride became pleasant. The hard parts were all done. They'd found the herd, they'd rescued it, and they had it all going in the same direction. They could relax a bit.

"What was with Gary back there?" Christine asked Stevie in a low voice. "I thought he was with you."

"I think I'm going to give up trying to figure out Gary Finnegan," Stevie said.

"A good thing, too," said Carole. "When you really could have used a hand, he decided he was more useful sitting in the saddle at the top of the hill watching cars!"

"Actually, Carole, I think he *was* more useful watching cars than he would have been rounding up strays," Stevie said wryly.

The truth of that statement overwhelmed Carole. She couldn't help herself. She burst out laughing.

To cover Carole's guffaws, Stevie began singing, " 'I'm a-headin' for the last roundup!' "

As she had suspected, that made Gary begin to sing too. Stevie let him take over. Singing was the one thing he really did well.

BY THE TIME they neared the Bar None, the young riders had figured out what they were going to do—eat. It was almost four-thirty, the sun was setting, and they hadn't had a bite all day. They had also decided they would put the stolen herd into the large paddock by the Bar None and keep the horses there overnight. They could be sorted out the next day when there was enough light to identify the brands. For now the herd was safe, and that was all anybody needed to know.

The horses followed their rescuers into the paddock and eagerly accepted the grain and hay the girls brought out for them. By the time the girls were done tending the horses, many of them were beginning to doze on their feet. The girls were ready for some of the same.

"Kate Devine! What's going on here?" Phyllis asked, running out from the kitchen. "Where have you been? What are you doing with all these horses? These aren't all ours! I'm sure I saw the Westerlys' brand on one. And look, that's the brand from the Double L! Why have we got their horses in our paddock?"

"It's a long story, Mom," Kate said. "And I think if you'll find something to feed us, we'll be able to tell you everything."

"Between bites," Stevie said. She didn't want any misunderstanding about exactly what was going to come first. She also didn't think anybody would be able to hear anything she had to say over her rumbling stomach.

The five girls and Gary followed Phyllis into the house, with Kate assuring her at every step that the horses belonged in their paddock for the night and would be safe there. Everybody—even the Westerlys and the Double L people—would be glad about it, Kate promised her mother.

Lisa was the last one through the kitchen door. She turned to pull it shut behind her and took one final look out at the herd they'd rescued. The last thing she saw was the two dun mares and the chestnut gelding. In spite of the fact that they had to be tired from their long trip, one of the mares was playfully nuzzling the gelding. Lisa could have sworn that the mare was tagging the gelding. "You're it," she whispered. She drew the door shut.

A big pot of chili was on the stove, kept warm for them since lunch. Phyllis filled six bowls and poured milk. The girls and Gary picked up their spoons and took their first bites since dinner the night before. Food had never tasted so good.

"Okay, that's four mouthfuls each. Now talk," Phyllis said.

They did. Kate did most of the talking, and she didn't say anywhere near as much about the wild-goose chase that Gary had led them on as Stevie would have said. In fact, Kate didn't say anything about it at all. She just said they'd finally figured out that the horses would most likely be near the old railroad spur and that they had actually found them there.

"We rescued them!" Gary announced proudly.

"Yes, *we* did," Christine said.

Carole explained how they'd taken the herd to the top of the hill and over to the high meadow and safety. Stevie described the runaway six and her total failure as a roper.

Gary looked puzzled. "I didn't realize you didn't know how to rope a horse," he said. "I could have done that for you."

"I'm sure," Stevie said.

Lisa had never thought of Stevie as a master of

understatement, but right then she thought Stevie deserved an award. Nobody contradicted her.

"But what about the people you think stole the horses?" Phyllis asked.

"They weren't there," Gary explained. "The girls thought they were coming back right away, but they weren't. It wasn't their car."

"Gary? Are you all right?" The front door of the lodge slammed shut behind Mr. and Mrs. Finnegan. They ran over to Gary.

"What happened?"

The girls were touched by the Finnegans' genuine concern for Gary—until Mrs. Finnegan's next question.

"You didn't hurt your hands, did you?"

"No, Mom, they're fine," Gary said. "Maybe a little tired from gripping the reins, but no problem. Really."

"Don't worry, Mrs. Finnegan," Stevie said. "I saw to it that nothing happened to Gary."

"Yeah, right, like she wouldn't let us abandon him on a mountain slope the way we wanted," Christine whispered to Lisa. Lisa stifled her giggles.

There was a loud thumping on the front porch of the lodge, and the door opened. Frank came in, followed by six other men. Phyllis and Kate greeted them by name. One was the sheriff and another was Mr. Westerly. The rest were other local ranchers.

"I suppose you haven't had anything to eat all day,

either, and you'll be glad to tell me what's going on as soon as you have a bowl of chili?"

"How'd you know?" Frank asked.

"There's a lot of it going on around here," said Phyllis.

The men hung up their coats and joined the six young riders at the Bar None's ample dining table.

"It's horse thieves all right," Frank said. "We found them in the cabin by the railroad spur. The sheriff's been trying to get the truth out of those men all day."

"You've got them?" Stevie asked, unable to contain herself.

"Well, we've got them," the sheriff said. "But I'm not sure we can keep them. At the moment they're guests of the town on the grounds of vagrancy. It's the darnedest thing. We know they've stolen horses, but we can't find the horses! All we could see was a mass of hoofprints, this way and that, in the corral and around the house, but it was getting dark so we couldn't follow them. It didn't make sense, anyway, since it was clear they intended to skedaddle out of here on the train tracks, and the hoofprints were leading away from there. Best we can figure is that they were looking for a place to hide them overnight."

"Uh, Dad," Kate said.

"We'll get them," Frank said. "Tomorrow morning, first thing, we're going back to that railroad spur, and we'll follow the trail on horseback."

"Dad—" Kate began again.

"We can put these folks up for the night, can't we, Phyllis?" Frank asked, not waiting for an answer. "That way we can head out early."

"Dad," said Kate.

"We've just got to find the herd. Without the herd, we don't have anything," said Mr. Westerly.

"No matter how far we have to ride," Frank agreed.

"True. But that herd could be days from here by the time we locate them," said the sheriff.

"Dad!" Kate said.

Mr. Devine turned to his daughter. "Honey, we men have some planning to do here. Can it wait?" he asked gently.

"I just thought you'd like to know that the herd is in our paddock," she said. Then she grinned.

"Our what?"

"That's what Kate's been trying to tell you," Phyllis said. "The girls brought the herd back here."

"*Gary* and the girls, you mean," said Mrs. Finnegan. She smiled at Gary, and he gave her a thumbs-up sign.

The sheriff gulped. "You mean to tell me that you kids went and stole a herd of horses?"

"From horse thieves," Kate said. "And yes, that's exactly what I'm telling you."

"I think I'd better take a look for myself," said the sheriff.

After the chili pot had been scraped clean, The Saddle Club took the sheriff and his posse out to the corral to see the herd of tired but safe horses.

"I think you'd better start from the beginning," said Frank as they returned to the main lodge.

"It all began when I picked up the phone, which I shouldn't have . . . ," Lisa began.

The men didn't interrupt until the rescuers finished describing how they'd given the hungry herd a welcome-home feed.

"Your guests seem mighty partial to the welfare of horses," the sheriff said.

"We are," Stevie responded, beaming with pride.

"And they may very well have saved these horses from an ugly fate. I'm sure those rustlers had the wherewithal to move the horses out before we got there. They must have been a touch surprised when they returned to the cabin and found the horses gone."

"I bet they were," Carole said gleefully.

"Well, you may have saved the horses, but there's been some damage done to the evidence," said the sheriff. "See, without the horses being there—that's called possession—it's going to be very hard to prove they were actually stolen in the first place by the men we have in custody."

"I never thought of that," said Stevie.

"But I don't understand," Christine said. "We took the horses from the same place you found the men."

"I know it's logical. We know they did it. We're just shy of a way to prove that those two men were ever anywhere near any of those particular horses," the sheriff said.

Kate spoke up. "We saw them on our land the other day. And actually, we stole the horses that we had seen them riding. They're in our corral, too."

"But no horses had been stolen the other day. The men *were* trespassing. But that's not the same thing as horse thieving. We need some evidence that will put them with the stolen horses before they were stolen."

Lisa gasped. She stood up and stuck her hand into her jeans pocket.

"Would this do?" she said, offering the sheriff three cigarette butts. "I found them in the feed tent by the Bar None herd. Aren't there some kind of scientific tests to show who smoked them?"

The sheriff slapped his knee. "Are you kidding? Get me a plastic bag! Boys, I think we've found a way to jail those horse thieves!"

Lisa grinned. That made the day perfect—well, almost perfect.

"Gary, I'm so proud of you!" said Mr. Finnegan. "You know, your mother and I were upset about your missing practice time this afternoon, but it looks as if you were up to something more important—for today anyway."

"That's right, Gary," said Mrs. Finnegan. "I guess the girls owe you a note of thanks for coming up with such a great idea. Saving horses and catching thieves—*say*, that might make a nice ballad, don't you think, Floyd?"

"Could be," said Mr. Finnegan.

"Son, shall we go work on it?"

"Sure thing, Dad," Gary said. He stood up to leave with his parents.

Frank and the sheriff and the other men went into the office to use the telephone, which was working again. The girls were alone. After a moment of quiet, Carole turned to Lisa.

"I guess I need to thank you," she said.

"I guess I need to apologize," said Lisa.

Nobody asked what either of them meant. They all just sighed with relief.

17

MORNING CAME VERY early the next day. The girls were still tired from their long ride the day before, to say nothing of the long celebration that had followed in the evening. Each of them was sure she could have slept another six hours, but it was almost dawn and this was their last day at the Bar None. They weren't going to miss out on their last dawn bareback ride.

"Everybody ready?" Stevie asked.

"Ready," her friends said. They'd dressed in the darkness and had bundled up warmly.

Stevie opened the door. More accurately, Stevie tried to open the door. It was frozen shut. It took three of them to get it open, and when they finally succeeded they knew they shouldn't have bothered. There was a four-foot wall of snow on the other side.

"We're snowed in!" said Kate.

"Let's go back to bed," said Stevie. "We can ride later."

"Like *really* snowed in," said Christine.

"I'm ready for another couple of hours of z's," said Carole. "We've got a long day ahead of us, because we're flying out of here after lunch, and then it's a couple of hours in the air."

"And tonight is the Starlight Ride," Lisa said. "Maybe it's just as well that we'll get more rest now."

The five sleepy girls each took off a couple of layers of clothes and happily climbed back into bed. Lisa's last thought as she drifted back to sleep in the predawn darkness was that she'd had a wonderful and exciting time at the Bar None—if she didn't count sticking her nose into Carole's business with Gary—but she was happy to be going home. Tomorrow was Christmas. Pot roast for dinner tonight.

Carole pulled the covers up to her ears. Her mind was filled with thoughts of the horses safe in the Bar None corral. Her thoughts drifted to her favorite horse, Starlight. She'd see him tonight. She'd hug him tonight. She'd ride him tonight. And tomorrow was Christmas . . .

Stevie pounded her pillow and then put her head on

it. A little more sleep was a good idea. She would need her strength. Tonight, back home, was the Starlight Ride. And she was going to be in the lead! She'd joked with Max about playing Follow the Leader and she mostly didn't mean it, but she was going to have fun, and so was everybody else. And then tomorrow was Christmas. Her last thoughts were of mounds of presents collecting underneath the Lake family Christmas tree, and some of them were for her!

These were the stuff their dreams were made of. The girls slept.

"Hello! Anybody there?"

There was a knock at the door. Stevie sat up abruptly, knocking her head on the bunk above her.

"Ouch!" she cried.

"What?" Carole said through a sleepy haze.

"Good morning!"

Lisa opened her eyes. Bright sunshine streamed through the cabin windows. She looked at her watch and then blinked. It was eight-thirty and somebody was knocking at the door.

"Who's at the door?" Carole asked.

"More important, how did someone get to the door?" Stevie asked, rubbing her head.

"You girls ever going to wake up?" asked the voice from outside.

It was John Brightstar. Lisa forgot she was already

dressed and instinctively pulled the covers up higher. "Good morning!" she said.

"Well, is that all the thanks I'm going to get for digging you out?"

"Come on in," Kate said.

John opened the door. He had managed to get snow all over himself in the effort of digging a path.

"I think it's the abominable snowman disguised as John Brightstar," said Christine.

"No, it's the other way around," John said, shaking snow onto the floor. "Because I don't think Mr. Abominable would bother to tell you that there is a distinct odor of French toast and bacon coming from the kitchen at the main lodge, and those who want breakfast should find a place at the table before the lady who runs the joint stops serving at nine o'clock."

Five fully dressed girls bounded out of bed, thumping loudly as they landed on the floor of the cabin in their stocking feet. They yanked on their boots and coats and dashed out of the bunkhouse.

"Thanks for digging us out!" Lisa said.

"My pleasure," John said, closing the door behind her. And then, before he returned to the stable, he said to her, "See you later."

She nodded. She definitely wanted to save a few minutes to say good-bye to John before they went home that afternoon. She'd go over to the barn after breakfast.

A stack of French toast and large glasses of fresh orange juice welcomed the girls to the table.

"Help yourselves," said Phyllis as she placed a platter of bacon in front of Stevie.

"And what are the rest of you having?" Stevie said, taking a large serving for herself.

"Very funny," said Kate. She took some bacon and passed the platter around to everyone else.

"Well, good morning!" Frank Devine greeted the girls. He sat down and poured himself a cup of coffee, but turned down the offer of breakfast.

"I ate hours ago," he said. "It's been a busy morning here while you girls were lolling around in your bunks."

"What's been happening?" Lisa asked curiously.

"Well, a number of things, and they all seem to concern you girls," Frank said. "First and foremost, I spoke with the sheriff about our horse thieves—or should I say, *your* horse thieves? Anyway, he said that last night he went back to town and he and his deputy had a few conversations with that pair. They explained to them about the herd of horses that had been rescued by 'reliable witnesses,' and he could see that the thieves were getting nervous."

Stevie grinned. "I bet he really made them sweat!" she said.

"They tried to shrug it off, saying there may have been some horses at the cabin or there may not, no matter what reliable witnesses said, but there was nothing saying that they had anything to do with the horses," said Frank.

"I wish I could have been there," Stevie said. "I could have wrung a confession out of those varmints!"

"Well, for all practical purposes, you did," said Frank. "Or, more accurately, *Lisa* did."

"Me?" Lisa asked.

"The cigarette butts!" Stevie declared. "It worked!"

"It worked, all right," Frank said. "The sheriff started out talking about the coincidence of the fact that those were the very same brand one of those guys smoked. They tried to wiggle out of that. But when the sheriff got to talking about things like fingerprints and DNA evidence, the two crooks totally fell apart. They knew they were goners and they confessed everything."

"Yahoo!" Stevie said.

"They gave the name of the guy who apparently masterminded the whole scheme, and the sheriff set plans into motion that could end up capturing a whole ring of horse thieves. Those cigarette butts didn't just save fifty horses—they may put a half dozen men in jail!"

"Is there a reward?" Stevie asked.

"Stevie!" Lisa said. "I don't care about that!"

"I'm just asking." Stevie shrugged. Her imagination tended toward chests of gold and jewels. Her friends often had to curb that kind of thinking on Stevie's part.

"No, no reward that I know of," said Frank.

"Knowing that we saved those horses is all the reward we need," said Carole, speaking for all of them, Stevie included.

"Well, maybe there's no reward, but there will be a celebration tonight, and Phyllis and I will be proud to host it," Frank said.

"Too bad we won't be here," said Lisa. "But take lots of pictures and send them to us, won't you?"

"Well, that's the other thing you've been sleeping through," he said.

"What?" Carole asked, suddenly suspicious that this might not be as good as the first news Frank had told them.

"We had about fifteen more inches of snow here last night. A lot of the range is clear because the snow drifted across the open spaces. John claimed that most of it seemed to drift up against your cabin door! I'm not sure about that, but the fact is that most of the rest of the ranch is passable. It appears, however, that whatever didn't drift up against your cabin door drifted onto the runway at the airport. Or maybe it just snowed harder there. That happens, too. They are reporting two feet of snow with drifts of up to eight feet."

"Wow. It must have been hard for them to get the place open," said Carole.

"Turns out, it was impossible," said Frank. "They can't get it open. It's totally snowbound."

"Are you saying *snowbound?*" Stevie asked. Frank nodded.

The word sank in.

"Until when?" Lisa asked, gulping.

"A couple of days at least. I think it should be clear by Friday."

"But that means . . . ," Lisa began. She couldn't finish. Everybody knew what it meant. It meant no pot roast for Lisa's Christmas Eve dinner. It meant no eggs Benedict for Stevie Christmas morning. It meant no Kwanzaa *kinara* for Carole Christmas night. It meant no presents and no Christmas at home.

"I've spoken with your folks," said Frank. "You can all call them whenever you want to, but I wanted them to know about the change in plans right away. Stevie, your mother said she didn't think she could keep your brothers away from their presents one second past dawn tomorrow, but she promised they'd have Christmas all over again on Saturday after you get home."

Stevie laughed. She could just see her brothers plowing into the pile of presents. It wasn't always a pretty sight. Maybe it was better to miss it after all!

"Carole and Lisa, your parents promised to hold everything until you get back."

"I guess there are advantages to being an only child,"

Lisa said, laughing. She often envied Stevie the rowdy bunch that were her brothers. But with only one child at home, it was easier to change the date of Christmas. Carole had similar thoughts.

"So, Phyllis and I would like to invite you all to have Christmas here at the Bar None with us and Kate and our other guests. You, too, Christine. You're welcome to stay. We'll try to make the holiday as special and as individual as everybody who's here."

"Since Stevie, Carole, and Lisa can't be with their families, I guess it's only fair if I stay here, too, and do what I can to make them feel at home," Christine said.

Kate looked at her four best friends and felt a glow of warmth. Being with friends was wonderful most of the time, but being with family on Christmas was important. She'd feel funny if she were in their place. But she also knew that her parents were wonderful at making Christmas right for everybody, no matter what their idea of "right" was.

"Don't worry," she said to her friends. "We'll make this Christmas special. We just have to figure out how to do it."

Stevie had an odd feeling. She loved being with Kate and she supposed it wasn't going to matter too much if she didn't have her actual Christmas until Saturday. That could wait. But there was something else that wasn't going to wait for her, something that might come only once in a lifetime. It was her favorite Pine Hollow tradition. She gulped when she realized what she was missing. Suddenly it was harder to be a good sport about being snowbound.

Carole glanced at her. In an instant she knew exactly what Stevie was thinking. But Carole hadn't spent years being Stevie's best friend without learning a thing or two from her.

"I say," she began. "Does anybody here have a torch?"

Stevie decided right then that she had the best friends in the whole world.

18

"HERE YOU GO, Stevie," Frank Devine said, handing her a torch. "In the summertime we use this to keep mosquitoes away from the picnic area. In the wintertime it seems like it will do very nicely for you to hold while you take the lead in the Bar None's newest Christmas tradition, the Starlight Ride!"

Carole and Lisa clapped loudly. If they couldn't be at the Pine Hollow Starlight Ride, then the next best thing was to bring the ride to the Bar None.

Back at Pine Hollow, the Starlight Ride sometimes had as many as thirty or forty riders. Here on the Bar None, it was just going to be the five members of The Saddle Club. They hadn't invited Gary, and he hadn't asked to come along. Nobody seemed in the least bit upset about that.

Stevie, Lisa, and Carole were on their horses. Kate and Christine were in a sled. Christine had pointed out that if they were going to take a ride, it would be a good idea to go back to where the main herd was and take some fresh hay with them. Frank Devine tucked blankets over their laps for warmth.

Walter had harnessed up a pair of horses to the flatbed sled, and John secured six bales of hay to the back.

"Drive carefully now," he said.

"We will," Kate said, flicking the reins. Much to her surprise, when the horses moved forward, the sound of tinkling bells rang out. Walter had found some sleigh bells and had attached them to the harness. It was just what the group needed to remind them of exactly what their mission was: fun.

Stevie took a deep breath. The crisp air filled her lungs. It wasn't even night yet. It was just past five o'clock, but it was already dark this time of year and that was an important part of the Starlight Ride. Five o'clock at the Bar None was seven o'clock at Pine Hollow. Two thousand miles away, another group of riders was doing exactly what The Saddle Club was doing: starting the Starlight Ride. Stevie smiled to herself.

There was something they were doing that night that wasn't part of the Starlight Ride, and that was checking on the herd. Earlier that day, Frank and his neighbors had sorted out the stolen horses. Frank had released his own horses back onto the range. John and his father had guided them toward the rest of the herd. Sometimes when herds split, it is difficult to get them to reunite. The girls told the Devines they wanted to be sure that they were getting along. They each knew that they just wanted a chance to see the horses they'd saved one more time before they returned home.

Stevie held the torch high. "Forward, ho!" she cried out. The ride began. She was followed by Carole, who had decided to wear a Santa Claus hat just in case anybody forgot that it was Christmas Eve; and then by Lisa, who found the whole scene breathtaking. Kate and Christine brought up the rear, their bells ringing brightly.

As soon as they got beyond the immediate area of the corrals around the Bar None, the snow became shallower.

"Sometimes it's like that out here," Kate explained. "The snow will be four feet deep around the ranch and little more than a few inches out here on the range. The wind pushes it around a lot, but it also falls in odd patterns. I guess it has to do with the mountains."

"Don't care what causes it," Stevie said. "I'm just glad we can ride and the horses can make it through."

They could. In some ways the trail they were blazing through the fresh-fallen snow was a familiar one. After all, they'd traveled out to the horse herd three times since they'd arrived at the Bar None on Sunday. But each time it had been different. The time of day, the light from the sky, the snow on the ground—everything combined to make each trip unique. Tonight it was dark, but there were no clouds. The sky above was an enormous expanse of deep purple blue, studded with stars that sparkled like diamonds. It made the snow-covered world completely visible, amost as in daylight.

"Oh!" Lisa said. "It always surprises me when I see the sky out here."

"What's so surprising?" Christine asked.

"Well, all those sparkly things, for one," Stevie explained.

"When you live as close to a big city as we do, the night lights of the city reflect into the sky and obscure the stars," Lisa explained logically.

"To say nothing of the air pollution of a densely populated area," Carole added.

"So you don't see stars?"

"We see some, but not like this," Lisa said. "Oh, you can spot some of the constellations if you can get to a large open area, like a ball field. I can find the Big Dipper and Orion, but then—what's that?" she asked, scanning the sky.

"What's what?" Carole said.

"That," said Lisa. She pointed to the sky in front of

them. There were seemingly thousands of stars there, but one was brighter than all the rest.

"You're the expert on the night skies," said Carole.

"It's not part of Orion or the Big Dipper," said Lisa. "At least I don't think it is." She looked around the sky. The bright star was nowhere near her familiar constellations.

"I bet it's the evening star," Stevie said.

"That's supposedly Venus, then," said Carole.

"Not necessarily," said Lisa. "At least I don't think it's always Venus. Evening star just means the first bright starlike thing that appears each evening."

"Aren't we supposed to wish on it, then?" Stevie asked.

"Sounds good to me," Carole said.

In unison the girls recited the poem:

> "Starlight, star bright,
> First star I've seen tonight,
> Wish I may, wish I might,
> Have the wish I wish tonight."

"What did you wish for?" Stevie asked.

"Can't tell or it won't come true," said Lisa.

"I think my wish already did come true," said Stevie.

"I'm glad we found a way for you to lead the Starlight Ride, even if we're not home," said Lisa.

Stevie smiled. Lisa was right about what Stevie had been wishing for.

The riders passed Parson's Rock and then took the turn that would lead them to the herd of horses. The snow remained relatively shallow, and Stevie could feel Stewball prancing through the whiteness. He was having as much fun as she was.

"There they are!" Stevie declared as the group reached the rise.

And there they were. A herd of more than fifty horses filled the meadow, standing and nibbling at an occasional stalk of frozen grass. Tails swished, hooves pawed at the snow. The moonlight gleamed across the white expanse and seemed to shimmer on the backs of the horses.

"Isn't that the most beautiful sight in the world?" Stevie asked.

"Yeah," Carole and Lisa agreed.

They fell silent as they watched the horses living free, under the star-studded night in the snow-filled meadow. It was utterly quiet because the snow on the ground muffled all the sounds except for the occasional whisper of the winter wind.

"Look, there are the dun mares!" Lisa finally said. The two horses were standing side by side, head to tail, apparently content. Just then, however, their peaceful moment was broken by the arrival of the frisky chestnut gelding.

He burst between them and frolicked across the field. The mares followed him.

"Tag! You're it!" Carole said, speaking for the gelding.

"Hey, let's unload the sled," Stevie said. It wasn't exactly that she was in a hurry to have the ride end, but Phyllis had said something about cocoa and marshmallows, and then there was dinner . . .

Kate and Christine drove the sled up to the lean-to, which was still standing. It was nearly empty, so the girls were glad they had brought more hay. Stevie dismounted, stuck the flaming torch into a snowbank, and grabbed one end of a bale. Christine took the other. They heaved it into the lean-to. Christine took out a knife and cut the wire. Stevie stood and waited.

A kind of grunting sound filtered into the lean-to. It startled Stevie because it didn't sound like anything she'd heard before. She listened. There it was again.

"What was that?" Stevie asked Christine.

"What was what?"

"That," said Stevie.

Christine heard it, too. "I don't know, but it sounds like a horse in trouble."

"That's what I thought. Let's go look."

The two girls headed toward the back of the lean-to. Carole, Lisa, and Kate had heard the sound, too, and they followed Stevie and Christine.

There in the shelter of the other side of the lean-to, a

horse was lying on her side in the snow, her legs splayed awkwardly. Even in the dark, they could see that the snow around her had blood on it.

"It's the pregnant mare!" said Lisa.

"And she's foaling!" said Stevie.

"Well, she's laboring to foal," said Carole.

"She's in trouble!" said Kate, and they all knew that was true.

"Well, then, we'll just have to help her," said Christine.

In an instant all five girls brought flashlights out of their pockets.

The girls had some experience in foaling, and they knew that the best possible situation was for the mare to do the whole thing without any help from humans. But there were times when the horse couldn't do it without help. The pained noises the mare was making told the girls this was one of those times.

"Look! A foot is coming out!" said Kate. The girls all looked where Kate pointed her flashlight. They could see a small white-covered object. It was the foal's front foot, still encased in the birth sac. The mother strained and heaved.

There should have been movement. There should have been more foot showing.

"She's not making any progress," said Lisa. "Is she going to be all right?"

"She is if I have anything to say about it," Carole declared.

Carole crouched down by the mare and waited. She could tell when the next contraction began by the way the mare was straining. But the horse was exhausted and, strain as she might, it wasn't helping the foal to come out.

Carole took hold of the foot and tugged. She didn't pull or yank. She just held it firmly, and when she could feel the contraction working to expel the foal, she helped by tugging ever so slightly.

"It's working!" Stevie said when the contraction stopped. "I'm sure there's more of the foot showing this time than last."

"I hope so," said Carole. The mare lifted her head, turning it toward the five girls. The look in her eyes was anguished. It touched Lisa's heart. She sat in the snow so that she could stroke the horse's face.

"It's okay, girl," she whispered. "We're here and we're going to help you. Nothing bad is going to happen if we have anything to say about it. My friend Carole, she knows what she's doing. She isn't exactly a vet; in fact, she's just a kid like me, but she's worked with a vet. She's helped a lot of foals be born. Come to think of it, I've helped once and so has Stevie. I bet Kate and Christine have, too. You're going to be okay and you're going to have a beautiful baby. We can already see the feet. Your baby has a white sock on one of its legs."

The mare closed her eyes and relaxed, calmed by Lisa's stroking and her voice.

When the next contraction came, the mare was strong enough to push hard. Carole was strong enough to pull hard.

"It's coming! It's coming. I can see some of the foal's nose now!" Carole announced. "But it's tiny, oh, so tiny. I've never seen such thin legs on a foal."

With the next contraction the foal's shoulders came out, and then something very odd.

"There are more feet!" Carole declared.

"Of course there are," Stevie said sensibly. "Most foals do have four."

"Not this one," said Carole, squinting to be sure she was seeing right. "This one has at least six!"

"Insects have six legs, not horses," Stevie said, irritated.

"Oh no," said Kate.

"What's the matter?" Stevie asked.

"It's twins. It has to be."

"Oh dear," said Stevie. Now she understood why the mare had been walking so uncomfortably with her pregnancy. One foal was a lot for a mare to carry. Two were an enormous burden.

The other thing Stevie knew was that this was bad

news. Twins were very rare in horses, much rarer than in humans. Most of the time twin pregnancies ended early in miscarriage. Sometimes one of the fetuses would be miscarried and the other might come to term and be born, but often when that happened the living foal wasn't a very healthy one. When two fetuses survived a pregnancy, it usually spelled disaster for the foals and often for the mare as well. Stevie was scared for this mare.

"I've got it!" Carole said. She held the legs tightly, and as the mare did what she could to help, Carole pulled. She could tell it was helping because the foal was moving toward her.

"Come on, girl, come on. You can do it!" Lisa whispered in the mare's ear. The mare looked up at Lisa, blinked, and then shuddered.

"It's out!" said Carole.

Lisa looked. The foal had been born all right. The little creature was encased in the sac and lay motionless in the snow next to its mother. Kate took a blanket from the sled and wrapped the inert little body in it. Then, using her pocketknife, she opened the sac. There was only the faintest chance that the foal had survived, but if it had, it would need air. The foal didn't move.

"Here's the other!" Carole declared. This one came out much more quickly. Before she knew what was happening, the second foal was lying in the snow where its sibling had been just moments before. Again there was no motion.

"How's the mother?" Christine asked.

Lisa stroked the mare's cheek and looked into her eyes. "She looks okay. She's tired, but okay," Lisa said. The mare put her head down and seemed to relax. In another minute she raised her head and pushed one more time, and the afterbirths were expelled.

"The babies?" Lisa asked, almost afraid, because she wasn't sure she wanted to know.

"I'm not sure," Kate said. "We've got both sacs open, but the foals aren't moving. It's hard to tell in the darkness. Ouch!"

"What was that?" Stevie asked her.

"That was a foal kicking me!" said Kate. "One of them is alive!"

The girls turned their flashlights on the now struggling little mass of wet brown fur. They watched it lift its head to take its first deep breaths of cool air.

"Ohhhh," said Carole. "It's so precious!"

"It's a girl!" Stevie announced.

"Let the mare see her filly," Christine said. The girls moved back and watched the mare touch her nose to the baby. The mare sniffed. The foal sniffed.

The scent of the newborn was just the tonic the mare needed to get her back on her feet. She nodded her head vigorously, shifted her weight forward, and in a matter of seconds was standing. Seconds later she was butting her newborn with her nose to get it to stand too.

The foal began to unfold her spindly legs. They splayed outward. The little baby seemed totally unable to control them. The mare licked her baby clean and dry while the baby worked to figure out why these long, awkward sticks were attached to her body.

The girls stood back and watched. They couldn't keep their eyes off the newborn foal. She was small but perfect and seemed to be in good health. The mother and daughter kept sniffing one another, and the mother licked lovingly.

"What was that?" Lisa asked.

"What was what?" Kate responded.

"I thought I heard something over . . . ," she began, looking at the place where they'd left the body of the second foal.

"Kate, it's moving," Lisa said.

"What's moving?"

"The second foal. It's alive."

"Oh, no way," said Kate. "It was still and stiff. I'm sure it didn't survive. It never happens, you know. Horses don't have twins."

"Maybe not, but it's Christmas Eve. That's a good time for a miracle, so you'd better take a look," Lisa insisted.

Kate looked. "Oh, get the blanket!" she said.

The girls turned their attention to see what Kate and

Lisa were looking at. By the time they did, the little foal's nose was sticking up out of the sac and reaching for life-giving air. They could see its nostrils flaring.

It didn't take long for the mare to realize that her second baby needed some attention, too. The girls stood back while the mother finished removing the sac and began sniffing the second foal. Soon the mare began her cleanup of the little one. The foal's tail flailed almost like a puppy's.

"It's happy!" said Lisa.

"Wouldn't you be, too?" asked Stevie.

"Definitely," Lisa agreed. "In fact, I am," she said.

Carole suggested that it would be a good idea for all of them to move back so that this new family could have a chance to get to know one another. They sat on the bed of the sled and watched.

It wasn't a fast process. Normally a foal would stand within a few minutes of birth, but this pair had had an unusually difficult birth, and because they were twins, each of them was unusually small. The girls reasoned that this pair had less control over their limbs than full-sized foals. However, like full-sized foals, they had a driving compulsion to stand up. Instinct told them that if they couldn't stand up, they couldn't get anything to eat, and food was definitely on their minds.

"What are we going to name them?" Stevie asked while they waited and watched.

"They're both fillies," Kate said.

"And it's Christmas Eve," Lisa said.

"Then there isn't really any question, is there?" said Stevie. "Their names are Holly and Ivy."

They didn't even have to take a vote. Stevie had gotten it exactly right.

"Holly and Ivy it is," Kate confirmed.

Holly, the firstborn, was the first one to make it to her feet. It took three tries before she could stay up, but she was undaunted. Once she was up, she looked over at her sister.

"I think Ivy is still trying to locate all of her legs and match them up with one another," Stevie observed.

"Persistence runs in the family," Carole said. "She'll do fine."

Carole was right. In a very few minutes Ivy was standing next to her sister. Both of them looked at their mother.

"I know that look," said Kate. "It's 'Okay, what's in this for us?'"

The mare stepped over to where her two babies waited patiently, as if she were trying to give them a hint about what would come next. They were quick studies. Seconds later the two of them were taking their first sips of nourishment.

Stevie sighed.

"I thought I wanted to be in Willow Creek tonight,"

said Lisa. "Now, I don't think I would have missed this sight for anything in the world."

"Me neither," said Carole.

"I think we should leave these guys alone now," said Kate. "John and his dad can come back for them in the truck later tonight. I think Mama and her babies will be spending the rest of this winter as barn horses. But for now, Mama's probably going to be hungry soon and she'll head into the lean-to. The babies will follow. They'll be warm enough in there."

As if the mare had heard, she walked into the lean-to with the babies stumbling after her.

The girls remounted their horses. Stevie picked up the torch. They began the return journey.

As far as they could see, mountains encased the land. Beyond and above, the starry sky arched protectively. Ahead of them, the moon laid a path to guide them. Behind them, the bright evening star stood watch over the snow-covered world.

19

"JINGLE BELLS, JINGLE bells, Jingle all the way!"

The girls were singing at the tops of their voices by the time they returned to the Bar None. It was an easy song for them to sing, inspired by the bells on the sled's harness. The horses seemed to prance to the music, such as it was.

Back at the lodge, the girls stepped into the warmth of a Christmas Eve celebration. The Devines, the Katzes, and the Finnegans were already gathered there. John and Walter had taken the horses and told the girls to go on in and get warm.

"You're not going to believe what happened!" Stevie said excitedly as she rubbed her hands together by the fire.

"Tell me you saved another herd of horses!" Mrs. Katz joked.

"No, just three," Carole said. "And they really needed saving, too."

"It was twins!" Lisa said.

"What *are* you talking about?" Phyllis asked as she handed out hot mugs of cocoa.

"Oh, Mom, it was something," Kate said. Everybody listened in rapt attention as the girls told the story and tried to describe the beauty of the knobby-kneed newborns. "In the end, the fillies were so tiny that they almost seemed to have to stand on tiptoe to get some milk," Kate finished.

"But they did it," Carole said.

"And we watched," Lisa added.

"And it definitely made this the best Starlight Ride ever!" Stevie said.

"Speaking of the Starlight Ride, didn't you girls say that part of the tradition is singing carols together while you have cocoa?" Mrs. Finnegan asked.

"By the town Christmas tree," Lisa said.

"Well, this isn't exactly a *town* Christmas tree," Frank said, pointing to the huge spruce in the main room of the lodge, "but it's the biggest one around. Want to give it a try?"

"Definitely," Carole said. She could see that the Finnegans had brought their guitars.

The Finnegans led everybody else in a few familiar carols, like "Hark, the Herald Angels Sing," and "Oh, Come All Ye Faithful."

Lisa loved to sing, and it was fun with such truly good musicians. Whatever her feelings about country-and-western music, she had to admit that the Finnegans knew what they were doing. It was a treat for everybody there. In years past, Lisa's favorite Christmas carol had always been "What Child Is This?" This year, however, the one that moved her the most was "Away in a Manger." Somehow the night's experience of helping in the foals' births and watching them take their first sustenance gave Lisa a new view on what the stable might have been like on that winter night so many years ago. When they sang "The stars in the skies looked down from above," Lisa looked at her friends. She knew they were all thinking the same thing. They were seeing the same stars she'd seen.

When the last strains of the song were finished, Phyllis announced that dinner was ready.

The Bar None guests followed their noses to the dinner table. They were greeted by a dinner that made Lisa gasp with pleasure and the Katzes grin with joy.

"It's pot roast!" Lisa said. "You remembered that that's what we always have! It's my Christmas Eve tradition!"

"That's not a pot roast. That's a brisket," said Ellen Katz. "It's a Hanukkah tradition!"

181

"It's both," said Phyllis. "It's two traditions in one, plus I've made what some people call potato pancakes and others call latkes, depending on whether it's a Christmas or Hanukkah tradition, I guess!"

"Whatever it's called, it smells wonderful!" Stevie said. "Can we start helping ourselves?"

"Please do," said Phyllis.

The guests passed the platters around, and for a moment there were few sounds except that of silverware clinking on plates. Then came the "mmms" and other happy noises.

"What's the significance of pot roast—er, brisket—and potato pancakes on Hanukkah?" Christine asked Ellen.

"It has to do with oil," Ellen explained. "The holiday celebrates the miracle of oil, recalling when there was only enough oil to burn in lamps for one night, but the short supply lasted eight nights. We light the candles in the menorah to remember that, but we also eat foods high in fat, like brisket, or cooked in fat, like latkes. Some say we do that to remember the oil in the lamps and I suppose that's true, but it's also a really good excuse to eat something our doctors might tell us isn't the best for us. Who can argue with religious tradition?"

Everybody laughed. Stevie reached for the latkes.

"Seconds already?" Carole asked.

"I have to have seconds," Stevie explained.

"Why?" asked Lisa.

"Because they come before thirds," Stevie reasoned, making everybody laugh.

After dinner came plum pudding—a Devine family tradition—and then it was time for the next part of the Hanukkah celebration: the lighting of the menorah.

The Katzes had brought their own menorah, one that had been in Fred Katz's family for generations. They asked the girls to put the candles in the holder and then asked Carole, who was the youngest person there, to light the shammes—the tall candle in the center—and to use it to light all of the other eight, each representing one of the eight nights of Hanukkah, while Fred and Ellen recited the traditional prayers in Hebrew.

When they were done, Carole told everyone more about the Kwanzaa candles she and her father always lit together.

The Finnegans sang a song called "Light One Candle."

Ellen spoke when the music was done. "I think this pair of newlyweds has just found a new Hanukkah tradition for our new life together. Thank you all for helping us celebrate."

"Our pleasure," Stevie said. "And besides, now you get a chance to help us do some celebrating. I saw a pretty tree over there. It's got a few strands of popcorn and cranberries on it, but I think it needs some other stuff, like lights, decorations, more garlands, and tons of tinsel. Will you help us?"

"I'll hold the ladder while you decorate the top!" Ellen offered.

It didn't take long before the bare spruce was totally covered with decorations. Some people might have thought that perhaps there were a few too many, but nobody at the ranch that night would have agreed. To those who helped and those who watched, it looked beautiful.

"Perfect!" Stevie declared, climbing down from the ladder.

The Finnegans, who had been singing "Deck the Halls with Boughs of Holly" while the others had climbed to perilous heights, put away their guitars and applauded the decorators. Stevie took a bow.

"The only thing that's missing is presents," said Carole. She'd meant it to be funny and her friends laughed, but it reminded them that they were away from their families and, no matter how much fun they were having, that was a little sad.

"Frank, would it be okay if I called my dad?" Carole asked.

"You don't have to, Carole," Phyllis said, coming out of the kitchen. "He's on the phone. He just called a minute ago. You two must have some kind of ESP!"

It turned out that it wasn't just Carole's father who

was on the phone. It was the Lakes and the Atwoods, too. Since Carole and Lisa weren't in Willow Creek with their families for the evening, the families had all gotten together at the Lakes' and were having a big, boisterous party.

The girls took turns talking to everybody. Stevie even talked to her brothers. She almost told them that she missed them. She said she did have presents for them and they could open them on Saturday when she got home, and if they hadn't gotten a present for her, well, the fact that Christmas would be two days late just gave them two more days to shop for her.

"You're shameless!" Lisa said to Stevie when the phone call was finished.

"You have to let them know what's right," Stevie said. "It's a sister's job."

"I'm surprised you didn't post your dress and sweater sizes on the bulletin board," Carole said.

"No, of course not," said Stevie. "I put those up in their bathroom, along with a list of the CDs I want."

Once again Lisa found herself wondering about the advantages and disadvantages of being part of a large family.

Her thoughts were interrupted by an announcement from Phyllis Devine, telling everybody they were to go to their bunkhouses and find a sock to hang up by the fireplace.

"*Clean* socks," Phyllis called after The Saddle Club.

A few minutes later each guest hung one sock on a nail on the mantelpiece, identified by a name tag so that Santa wouldn't get mixed up.

"Now, the next Devine family tradition is Christmas morning in pj's and bathrobes. Nobody has to get dressed up. Breakfast at nine. And before we go off to bed, I hope the Finnegans will sing us one more carol."

Phyllis began turning out the lights in the lodge until the room was lit only by the lights on the Christmas tree and the flickering candles on the Katzes' menorah.

Gary picked up his guitar and began strumming softly.

" 'Silent night,' " he began. Everybody joined in.

When the last note was sung, the guests turned to go to their rooms. The girls filed out the front door and walked through the cold night under the star-filled sky to their cabin. At last they slept.

"LAST ONE TO the lodge is a rotten egg!" Stevie declared at eight-thirty the next morning. "I've got to see what's in my stocking!"

It didn't take long for the girls to get ready. They brushed their teeth, donned bathrobes, and pulled boots on over their socks.

"Merry Christmas!" They were greeted at the door by pajama-clad revelers. The house was filled with the welcoming smells of breakfast, and the mantelpiece seemed to buckle under the weight of twelve overstuffed socks.

"Take me to my goodies!" Stevie declared. Everybody agreed it was time to see what Santa had brought.

Each sock had an apple or an orange in it, some candies, a candy cane, and a little something special.

Stevie got a Slinky; Carole got a little picture puzzle of a horse; Lisa got a game in which she was supposed to get all the silver balls into the center of a maze. Santa had brought Christine a pellet that, when put into water, was supposed to make a magical crystal world. Nothing was very fancy, but everything was fun and given with love and care.

Carole gave all the Devines a hug to thank them for making it one of the best Christmases ever. They hugged her back.

"You're a good part of what's making it so special for all of us—you and your dude friends over there!" Frank said.

Then Phyllis announced that breakfast was ready.

"You remembered!" Stevie said when she saw that the menu included more than Phyllis's traditional stollen. In the center of the table was a tray of eggs Benedict. Carole thought she saw a tear in the corner of Stevie's eye, but Stevie swiped at her face fast, so Carol wasn't sure. In any case, if it was a tear, it was one of joy, because Stevie attacked the breakfast with the same eagerness she always seemed to have for food. Of course, she began by scraping the hollandaise off the eggs.

"Just the way I like it," she said, grinning broadly.

When breakfast was over the guests returned to the main room and sat by the warm fire, enjoying one another's company.

Christine spoke. "Well, since this seems to be a time of mixed traditions, I think perhaps I should share, too. And since my grandfather has died and my mother isn't here, it falls to me to tell our family tale. My grandfather and my mother always began the story by saying they don't know if it's true. They only know that this is what our family has passed down."

Many years ago, before the first man was in this land, before the first animals walked in the meadows, before the first tree grew, before the first cloud touched the sky, there was a hawk. He flew the skies. He soared as high as the mountains. He dipped as low as the meadows. He never ate or drank and he never knew hunger, thirst, or pain. He knew only joy and curiosity.

One day, he became curious about the land beyond the mountains, and he flew to explore it. He found many wonders. He found other creatures of the land, the sea, the skies. He found trees and grass and flowers. But he longed for his own land. He flew home. It was as he had left it, and he was glad.

But as he soared over his own land, he dropped something from his talon. It was a seed that had become stuck in his claw when he was in the other land. The seed fell to the earth. It grew a root. It grew a tree. It grew grass. Flowers sprang up nearby. In the grass grew creatures and people of the land. In the tree grew birds of the air. In a stream fish flourished.

And all around the land, people grew strong and healthy,

feeding on the seeds and the animals of the land, drinking the water of the stream.

The hawk watched from above, and when he saw the wonders that had come to his land, he flew down to look. He saw a small creature and he took it for food. He saw the water of the stream and he drank it.

The people saw the hawk eating and drinking as he had never done before and they knew that the hawk had changed the land and the land had changed the hawk. And they saw that now the hawk needed the land. They would have to care for it evermore.

There was a moment of quiet when the story was done.

Ellen Katz was the first to speak. "Thank you, Christine," she said. "I think Fred and I may add *that* to our Hanukkah traditions as well!"

Everybody laughed.

"You know," said Lisa, "I'm having such a good time, I may never want to go home."

"Too bad," said Frank. "Just when I was about to tell you that the airport's going to be plowed and open early tomorrow morning."

"Well, on second thought . . ."

The girls didn't have to say it. This was fun, but home was home.

21

"RACE YOU TO the creek!" Stevie declared three days later.

It was Sunday afternoon. They'd been back in Willow Creek since Friday night, but the girls had barely seen one another since they'd gotten home. They'd been busy making up for missed time with their families and, as Stevie reminded them, there had been all those presents to open.

The girls had agreed to have their own Christmas at TD's that afternoon *after* a good ride.

"Can you believe how warm it is?" Lisa asked. They were all wearing sweaters and light jackets to counter the fifty-degree weather, a big change from the near-zero temperatures out West.

All three girls were glad to be back on their favorite horses. They each loved the horses they rode at the Bar None, but as far as Carole was concerned, Starlight was the best horse in the world. Stevie wouldn't have wanted to contradict Carole, but for her money Belle was number one. Lisa thought all horses were just fine, but for now she was happiest on Prancer. Prancer seemed glad to have her back. She was trotting in a style true to her name, too: She positively pranced across the field toward the woods.

It didn't take long to get to the creek. If it had been summertime, they would have taken off their boots and dangled their feet in the cool water. Today they had to be satisfied with perching on the big rock by the water's edge and watching the icy water slip past.

"It was great, but I'm glad to be back," Stevie said.

"Every trip to the Bar None is different in a wonderful way," said Carole. "I mean, this time it was Christmas and I loved getting to know the Katzes and the Finnegans."

Lisa gulped. She had something she had to say. It wasn't easy, but not saying it was going to be harder.

"Carole, I haven't apologized to you enough about butting in between you and Gary," she said.

"You were right," Carole told her. "I mean, he is a great singer, you can't deny that—"

"Really great," Lisa said.

192

"Right, but that's not enough. When the chips were down, Gary was a jerk. I was a fool to have had a crush on him. I need to thank you."

"No you don't," said Lisa. "Just because I saw something you didn't, didn't give me the right to stick my nose in. I'm never going to do that again."

"I promise I'll never get a crush on another jerk," Carole said solemnly.

"But if you do, I promise I'll tell *you*, not him," said Lisa.

"So, you think my boyfriend's a jerk?" Carole asked in mock anger.

Lisa laughed. So did Stevie and so did Carole.

"I think there's a lesson here," said Stevie. "If I've got this right, the lesson is that no boy is more important than our friendship."

That was something they definitely could agree on.

"And the other lesson is that if we don't get to TD's, I'm going to starve to death," Stevie said. TD's, short for Tastee Delight, was the ice cream shop where the girls often had Saddle Club meetings. "I nearly went into sundae withdrawal while we were at the Bar None. Are you girls ready for some *real* food?"

"I'm ready for a sundae," Lisa said. "But I hardly think those ghastly concoctions you order at TD's qualify as *real* food. Now, *real* food is hot caramel on—"

"Lemon ice!" Stevie said.

"Let's go," said Carole.

The girls took an extralong time grooming their horses and giving them treats. They needed to make up for the time they'd spent at the ranch. It was late in the afternoon by the time they settled into their favorite booth at TD's.

It didn't take long for the girls to order. Or at least it didn't take long for Carole and Lisa to order. Each wanted hot fudge on vanilla. Stevie, on the other hand, ordered one scoop each of pistachio and peppermint, strawberry and crème de menthe, with red and green sprinkles.

"And don't forget the cherry, right?" their usual waitress asked.

"Right," Stevie said solemnly. "Thank you."

"Don't you want any nuts on it?"

"No, this is a Christmas sundae," Stevie said. "Just red and green."

"I couldn't have figured that out on my own, even if I'd wanted to," said the waitress, retreating quickly.

Lisa and Carole laughed. Somehow Stevie maintained a straight face.

For a few minutes the girls discussed the drill their Pony Club would put on in a couple of weeks. It was hard to believe they'd been practicing just a day before their trip to the Bar None. It seemed like a lifetime ago. Then Stevie got a gleam in her eye.

"I think it's time for our presents," she said. "I mean, you guys may or may not have something for me, but I've got something for you."

With that she fished two identical packages out of her backpack.

"Me too," said Lisa. She took two packages out of the tote bag she was carrying.

"Me three," said Carole. She opened up a small box she'd been holding on her lap and put a package in front of each of her friends.

Stevie looked at the six packages sitting on the table and wrinkled her brow.

"What's the matter?" Lisa asked.

"Just look," said Stevie. "Six packages, all exactly the same size."

Carole and Lisa looked.

"Did you? . . ."

"At the mall? . . ."

"That wagon? . . ."

Stevie went first. She opened her gift from Carole. It was a small, beautiful glass horse.

"Really?" Lisa asked. She opened her gift from Stevie. It was the same thing.

"I can't believe this!" Stevie said, opening her gift from Lisa. A third glass horse stood on the table.

"It's beautiful!" said Stevie.

"I knew you'd like it," said Lisa.

"Me three," said Carole.

The girls each opened their other gifts, and then there were six glass horses standing on the table.

"I guess we know good presents when we see them at the mall," said Lisa.

"Or maybe we just know one another too well," Carole said.

"Maybe," said Stevie. "And here's the test. I know what I'm going to name my new horses. What about you two?"

"I've got an idea," said Lisa.

"Holly and Ivy," said Carole.

"That's *my* idea," said Lisa.

"Me three," said Stevie.

"Merry Christmas," announced the waitress, putting Stevie's sundae down in front of her.

"It is," Stevie assured her. Her friends agreed.

ABOUT THE AUTHOR

BONNIE BRYANT is the author of more than a hundred books about horses, including The Saddle Club series, The Saddle Club Super Editions, the Pony Tails series, and Pine Hollow, which follows the Saddle Club girls into their teens. She has also written novels and movie novelizations under her married name, B. B. Hiller.

Ms. Bryant began writing The Saddle Club in 1986. Although she had done some riding before that, she intensified her studies then and found herself learning right along with her characters Stevie, Carole, and Lisa. She claims that they are all much better riders than she is.

Ms. Bryant was born and raised in New York City. She still lives there, in Greenwich Village, with her two sons.